PRAISE FOR
RECO₂GNITION

"*ReCO2gnition* is a fast-paced sci-fi thriller that will have the reader pinned to their seat. Not only is the story entertaining, but it is also intellectually stimulating. The characters are fascinating and the narrative is colourful and detailed; Dowson uses words to paint pictures that are vivid and alive. Highest Recommendations!"

—JIM ARROWOOD, Sci Fi Blogger, jimsscii.blogspot.com

"*ReCO2gnition Oxygen Debt—Part 1*, is a suspenseful, futuristic tale that will keep you wanting more. Can it end up well?

"It is also interesting how the characters develop and how the story takes you to a future where devastation had taken place. The author describes future earth with no natural light, just smog clogging the sky and bright aero lights punctuating the dark sky. 2112 is a time where humans pursuit to immortality by adding human consciousness into advanced, lifelike machines. Leading to the creation of machines that could develop their own cognition. With such limited resources and life left, the only way to save the human race was Operation Reset. I can't wait to finish reading this book!

"People who enjoy science fiction books will find this a must-read."

—LUCIANE BARBOSA, Marketing Director at Wolf Digital Marketing Ltd, Book reviewer

"*Reco2gnition* is an intelligent, well-crafted thriller with great forward momentum, lots of intrigue and memorable characters."

—RADHA SPRATT, Editor of the South Asian Literature Festival's magazine and *The Marlowe Society Journal*

"Prepare to become a fan of Mark Dowson; in his debut novel he's created science fiction for the well-read. Mark skillfully interlaces subgenres, taking the reader through a mix of thrilling science fiction, political machinations, and romantic time travel."

"Science fact and science fiction collide in this eco-thriller from Mark Dowson. Two time travelers from 2112 return to the present day, one to assassinate a wind energy engineer, the other to rescue him—and perhaps save the planet!"

"As a screenwriter, I am currently adapting the trilogy into feature length films and we already have interest from a major US studio."

"Very impressed. The level of research that has clearly gone into this is mind blowing! A fascinating insight into a reality mankind might just be heading towards. Mark Dowson paints a vivid and thought-provoking image of the future. In Mark Dowson's *ReCO2gnition*, the future has been set . . . Can mankind change its fate?"

"A convincing portrayal of a potentially dark future, a clear warning that our current lack of commitment and reckless environmental behaviour can destroy nature and end our dream of a prosperous future.

"The vision and conviction of the author is not only outstanding but serious. The shorty line is effective in exploring new thinking and even technical solutions.

"It is promising to see that the new generation is taking environmental challenges seriously and trying to spread the idea through story telling."

—MAHTAB FARSHCHI, Course Director, University of West London

"If you like crime, mystery and romance all wrapped up in a sci-fi thriller, this is for you. Mark has also introduced today's global concerns as a crucial theme, and if that isn't enough, he's cleverly focused on mental health too. You'll need to concentrate, but that's its magic."

—GRAHAM MILLER, Public Relations Executive at Media-Vu, Media Consultant, Broadcaster at BBC News, Public Relations Advisor, Media trainer

"An intriguing juxtaposition of science fiction, science fact and fast-paced dramatic plot development set against the backdrop of one of the greatest challenges of our times—climate change. A hugely entertaining, relevant and stimulating read."

—DR. VOLKER BUTTGEREIT, CDir, PhD, DIC, M.Eng, ACGI, Managing Director, FD Global Limited, 'Designing Large Scale Building-integrated Wind Turbines for the World Trade centre in Bahrain'

"Sci-fi, ecosensitive, time-travelling thriller which alternates between the present and a post apocalyptic world where a leading scientific genius must be transported to the future to save humanity. Keeps you guessing to the end whether he will succeed or not."

—JAMES TUTTLE, Reviewer

"A great read. Time shifting and hi technology giving a vision of the 22nd Century if we let things continue as they are, not a pleasant vision of the future. Our thoughtful lead, Ben Richards leaves all the super hero stuff and the 22nd Century players. Having Part 1 in the title of the book suggests that our characters all have a long journey ahead of them in their attempts to save the planet. The book is mainly set in Italy around 2017 giving a reality about the story. The environmental issues of global warming are well discussed and the consequence of bad decisions clearly a warning for all readers. Each of the characters are well fleshed out and all the tech detail felt credible."

—ALASDAIR GIBSON, Sales Director, Mohn Media UK

RECO₂GNITION:
Oxygen Debt
Part I

by Mark Dowson

© Copyright 2019 Mark Dowson

ISBN 978-1-63393-889-2

Published by

 köehlerbooks™

210 60th Street
Virginia Beach, VA 23451
800–435–4811
www.koehlerbooks.com

RECOG$_2$NITION

OXYGEN DEBT
PART 1

MARK DOWSON

VIRGINIA BEACH
CAPE CHARLES

PROLOGUE

The early-morning sea was unusually calm as she swam gently, just breaking the surface with her glistening hair and shoulders. These moments were precious to her. When she was in the sea, nothing else mattered. She could clear her mind. She was confident in her body's buoyancy and felt that the sea would always protect her. All was peaceful, almost timeless—until she heard the shrieks.

A small child leaped up and down on the water line, arms waving. The frantic cries were high-pitched and desperate. The shore was deserted; only the swimmer witnessed the chaos.

The warning cries stopped just as the sky darkened.

CHAPTER 1

TIGHTROPE WALKER

JULY 4, 2017

As the sun set over the Arno River, Dr. Ben Richards adjusted his lens. He zoomed in on the man creeping along a tightrope parallel with the Ponte Vecchio far below his terrace. As the man made his way freehand towards a platform about 120 metres away on the north side of the river, Richards hit the shutter on his sleek, black DSLR camera, set to *continuous*.

Richards cast his mind back to an incident that occurred earlier that morning. Tragically, a delegate had collapsed and died right in front of him at a seminar he attended in Florence.

The man, thirty years Richards' senior, had been sitting just three rows in front of him. Professor Towriss had devoted his career to the wind-farming industry. He was one of more than 200 people who had packed the main auditorium of the historic University of Florence's Institute and Museum of the History of Science to hear the keynote speech of Professor Adam Robertson, head of the University of Glasgow's Environmental Change and

Society Research Programme.

·   Towriss had an apparent seizure shortly after Professor Robertson announced that all work in the field related to large-scale onshore and offshore wind farms was about to become obsolete, superseded by cheaper, more efficient methods of generation. Afterwards, some people seated near Towriss reported that the professor had looked distressed and was sweating heavily as Robertson undermined Towriss' life's work.

Robertson explained how most of the energy yield from large wind farms was lost from the point of generation to the end user. Much of Robertson's argument was based on the unpredictability and inconsistency of blustery offshore winds, and the propensity of air masses in vast, open spaces to change direction and create wind shear and turbulence in the vicinity of turbines.

As he stared through his camera, Richards wondered about the inconsistency of the breezes issuing from the Arno and what might happen to the tightrope walker if he were to experience sudden and unexpected turbulence. But mostly Richards reflected on how cruel life could be, and on the utter unpredictability of fate.

Professor Towriss was a committed and respected member of the academic community, and in an instant his life's work was obliterated, reducing him to an old man gasping for breath and fighting for his life. Sadly, it was a fight that he was destined to lose.

Richards was contemplating Towriss' legacy in the field of sustainable energy generation when his train of thought was broken by a sudden change in the light as the sun disappeared behind a cloud and then re-emerged. As if distracted by the shifting light over the river, the man on the tightrope paused. Richards lowered the camera. He glanced to his right and saw tourists funnelling up the tree-lined avenue to the Piazzale Michelangelo above the river. Others were already standing on the square, pointing up at the tightrope. The upturned faces in the crowd glowed in the golden light bathing the piazza.

Richards lifted his camera again, training his eyes on the man, who had begun again his careful choreography. It was only then that Richards noticed what the funambulist was wearing. The man was dressed from head to foot in the livery of a court jester. He had a well-worn cap with what looked like ass ears protruding from each side. Beneath that, his motley was a patchwork of alternating gold and black squares. One of his tights was black, the other gold. On his shuffling feet the man wore black leather shoes curled up at the toes.

"It's a panorama worthy of Titian, is it not?"

The voice startled Richards and came from a white-suited man with thick and unkempt black hair, raven eyebrows, an impressive moustache and a short beard.

"What's it all about?" Richards asked.

"It's a festival of what you English call *folly*. In our language *buffoon* means 'a bag of wind.' We love to make fun of the windbags."

The man chuckled before drawing an MS cigarette from a white-and-gold packet with red and black letters. He offered one to Richards, who frowned and shook his head. As the end of the cigarette began to glow, Richards noticed words engraved on the side of the solid-gold lighter: *SATOR AREPO TENET OPERA ROTAS*

"Forgive me, but what does that mean?'

"It's Latin," the man said. "Its origin and translation are disputed."

"But what do you think?" Richards asked.

The man was about to answer when there was a gasp from the crowd.

Richards turned back to the river below and looked through his viewfinder. The jester was now juggling four gold and black balls.

"He is a brave man, I'll give him that," Richards murmured.

"Quite so," the man on his left said, exhaling a white cloud.

Richards peered at the jester tiptoeing towards the orange terracotta rooftops just beyond the finishing platform. As he did, the shadows below thickened just as a thin shaft of light penetrated the clouds above, catching the jester in a moment of intense illumination. Richards hit the shutter button.

He was about to turn back to his new acquaintance when the crowd gasped again. He refocused his Olympus with a shaking hand.

"Oh no," he cried.

A sudden gust of wind had blown across the river. The tightrope was now shaking like a washing line, and the jester, who no longer had a wide smile, tried desperately to regain his balance. He dropped all of his juggling balls, which fell haphazardly towards the meandering river below, and stretched his arms out like wings.

For a moment it looked like he would fall. But as suddenly as it had arrived, the wind died down, causing the wire to become tense again.

Richards sighed.

"He's going to make it."

But just as the jester started to take a few tentative steps, he froze. He opened his mouth in shock and clapped at his neck as if he'd been stung by a wasp. There were gasps. A woman cried aloud.

Then someone began to scream. The jester's body seemed to atrophy as he fell clumsily onto the rope, which caught his fall before tipping him headfirst into the river below. Richards' heart throbbed.

The crowds behind Richards pushed forward, desperate to see the cause of the clamour. Richards braced his back against the surge and lifted his head from the camera, gazing wide-eyed at the jester, whose limp and gaudy form was now about to submerge beneath the surface of the river. Richards leaned over the railings on the terrace and tried to raise his camera to make use of the zoom, but his arm was caught in the crush of the spectators.

"Here!"

The man in the white suit grabbed hold of his trapped left arm and forced it free. In a swift movement he raised the camera in front of Richards' eyes and over his face.

"Thanks," Richards muttered as he took the camera and hit the shutter release button.

"*Prego*," the man replied.

Richards caught his breath again and gazed through the viewfinder. A white motorboat with a fluttering Italian flag had reached a point near the Ponte Vecchio, and several men in black wetsuits and fins tipped backwards into the river. A few moments later the sound of clapping began as the jester, now hatless, was brought coughing and spluttering to the side of the boat.

The relieved onlookers on the piazza lit cigarettes and dispersed towards the restaurant behind. Richards was about to turn when something caught his eye through the viewfinder; he noticed a scratch on the lens. Richards rubbed his eyes and then wiped the zoom lens with a handkerchief. He swivelled it back and looked through the electronic eyepiece. It was still there.

"Damn!" he cried.

He looked left, but the bearded man had gone.

Richards reached for his camera bag on the ground and retrieved the cover for the zoom lens. As he knelt to screw it on, he saw something near his left shoe. Next to the smouldering butt of an MS cigarette was what looked like a red-winged dry fly, the kind a fisherman would use to lure trout—only it wasn't a fly. It was a tiny dart from a high-powered rifle.

CHAPTER 2

CRISIS

FEBRUARY 2112

O ver the previous decades, more and more of the earth's surface had become unfit to live on, yet the population continued to grow rapidly. The effects of global warming over the past 200 years extended the arid zone of North Africa far to the north and the south, into Europe. The Alps and Pyrenees had become barren of any crop growth, in spite of the best efforts of agricultural science. The resulting mass migrations of people brought the great cities of Western and Northern Europe to their knees, with the demands of feeding and housing a bulging populace far exceeding the capacity of economy and infrastructure.

The Americas were in a similar state, with deforestation of the Amazon basin turning the central core of South America into a denuded and polluted wasteland. Its coastal cities suffered from extreme poverty and overpopulation, having been the target of migrants for several decades. The Eastern Seaboard and Midwest of what used to be the United States of America remained uninhabitable after the global nuclear conflict of the mid-twenty-second century, which also made uninhabitable the land formerly settled in the Middle East of Eurasia, and the entire expanse of Europe's former industrial heartland east of the Baltic.

With the hopelessly overpopulated continent of Africa long since abandoned to disease, starvation and tribal warfare, the only parts of the world where human existence was viable were areas controlled by the Confederation of Australasia (CoA), the parts of North America's West Coast that lay between the Rocky Mountains Military Exclusion Zone (RMMEZ) and the vast Pacific levees constructed to combat rising sea levels, and coastal Antarctica. Even the advanced urban city-regions of Far East Asia had succumbed to a series of urban population explosions. Little was known of what human life remained there after the mass exodus to Australasia during the 2080s and 2090s.

Throughout what remained of the civilised world, martial law had become the norm, as it was the only way to control the rationing of scarce food and the final dregs of the world's supply of uncontaminated fossil fuels.

The highest political and legal authority in the world was the United Nations Authority (UNA), which was based in Melbourne, CoA. Established 167 years previously as simply the United Nations, the UNA's original purpose had been to preserve world peace by preventing the outbreak of world wars like those that had blighted that century. The UNA's role was to abate scourges threatening civilisation, such as the very real prospect of food and power shortages.

A major and telling outcome of the global nuclear conflicts was that the fossil fuels that drove human development through the twentieth century and the first half of the twenty-first century lay in regions of the world that were now too radioactive and toxic for the exploitation of the dwindling resource. The UNA had therefore pinned its hopes on the development of genetically modified (GM) crops that could be grown in arid conditions, and power generated in enormous nuclear reactor plants. Unfortunately, the trust placed in biotechnology and GM crop science was misplaced. Insects mutated and adapted to the insecticides created by UNA's scientists. Vast regions of prairie land had been ravaged.

Another failure had been with the entity entrusted with power generation. The UNA granted a global monopoly to GIATCOM Corporation to provide the world with light and power for the foreseeable future. However, GIATCOM had been rocked by a series of attacks to its reactors during the early part of the twenty-second century—acts of sabotage by disgruntled employees, former employees, and political splinter factions that emerged after the dramatic global events of the 2040s and 2050s.

More recently, a new threat against the global power producer had emerged—the rise of religious sects based on fatalism. These extremists saw no hope for humans and the world, preferring instead to preach suicide and destruction. In the summer of 2110, an attack by one of these groups on a major GIATCOM installation on the North Island of what used to be called New Zealand convinced the UNA that the days of nuclear power—and therefore of what remained of the civilised world—were numbered. There was no scientific knowledge or infrastructure for alternative means of power generation.

· ·

It was in this grim context that Milton Westcroft, president of the UNA, chaired an emergency meeting of all directorates and departments of the executive council of the UNA in Melbourne, the capital of the CoA, on the twenty-ninth of February 2112. The sole purpose of this meeting was to discuss what, if anything, could be done.

For six hours, experts in every discipline had presented analyses of the situation—projections of future energy requirements of the world's population and the remaining resources available in UNA-controlled areas; the current security situation at the remaining installations; and a review of food requirements in relation to uncontaminated arable land resources.

The atmosphere among the delegates was sombre as no one felt either surprised or buoyed by the world's state. Rather, there was a solemn collective acknowledgement that the UNA executive council was obliged to formally set out the facts of the situation, to underpin and justify the monumental decision that might have to be made.

In the weeks and months leading up to the meeting, President Westcroft knew that there would be a strong representation from GIATCOM and from a fair number of extinction deniers who would argue for keeping faith with the nuclear programme. He also anticipated calls from the military hierarchy to tighten martial law in the CoA but understood that this would merely delay the exhaustion of resources and prolong the existence of an elite few. Others had begun to descend into fatalism, seeing little hope, regardless of any action that might be taken.

Westcroft knew one hope remained, something a small number of close political associates referred to as *Operation Reset*.

A woman in a red suit waited patiently as Westcroft looked out the window. A UNA android stood behind her, motionless and as straight as a cane, bright eyes burning into him, a picture of shining, chrome well-being.

A few decades earlier, it had been the aspiration of scientists to install consciousness into advanced, lifelike machines in pursuit of immortality. It hadn't worked. Organic brains needed organic bodies. Or so it seemed. Rival corporate technology giant GIATCOM, in a separate research programme, had begun developing androids that could shapeshift like chameleons using human implants. Unknown to the UNA, GIATCOM had also implanted some androids with human brain cells. The result was machines that could develop their own cognition.

President Westcroft mused that it had been almost twenty years since he looked out of a window to see a lush, green landscape. And here he was, standing half-stooped, hands clenched around the ancient oak gavel made from one of the last trees, staring out at the dead rainforest.

There was no natural light, just smog clogging the sky and bright aero-lights punctuating the filthy mists like small suns. There was no green except the neon sign he could just see glowing above the multi-mall by the decaying ruins of the grand opera house.

Figures moved far below, tiny, ant-like, all wearing oxygen masks. He touched the emergency canister clipped to his belt, knowing that windows could break and expose him to the contaminated air. There was an avenue in front of the council building. Once, there would have been dog-walkers and joggers. Westcroft's father had owned one of the planet's last dogs, a black Lab cross called Ninja. He missed dogs.

Westcroft ran his hands through his thinning grey hair. He was forty-five and one of the oldest people he knew and nearing the end of his life. His grandfather had lived to be ninety-six. He chuckled bitterly. What could he have done with an extra fifty years if by some chance it was offered to him?

"Mister President, sir."

Westcroft turned to face the woman in the red suit. She wheezed as she stood by the door. A scarf covered her hairless head, and her eyes sank into the greying skin of her browless sockets. She was in her mid-twenties but already looked almost as old as he. *Popcorn lung,* he supposed. That's what got most of them. Or a cancer.

"The council has come to a decision," said the woman.

"And what is that decision?" asked Westcroft.

"The council has voted in favour of setting in motion Operation Reset."

He turned his back on the window and followed the woman into a high-ceilinged auditorium. They had reached a decision, but many animated discussions still raged. President Westcroft took his position behind the large, raised table that was symbolic of the high status of his office.

"Ladies and gentlemen," he began. "Ladies and—can I have some order, PLEASE!" he bellowed, hammering the gavel on its block with such force that it broke into several pieces. The sound of oak fragments tinkling on the polished marble floor silenced the delegates.

"Ladies and gentlemen," he announced once again. "We have a statement from the council's secretary."

Phoebe Lomax, the woman in the red suit, approached the microphone. She paused and then began a carefully worded statement that had just been drafted.

"Let it be recorded that this emergency meeting of the executive council of the United Nations Authority has listened to the arguments presented by President Milton Westcroft, and to the various counter-arguments that have been put forward." She stopped to regain her breath. "We have considered all of the points raised, with great care. This council bears a heavy burden of responsibility for this gift that we now have, and it is our conviction that the time portals should never be used lightly. Nobody here needs to be reminded of the consequences of the Riaz Affair in 2088."

As he listened, Westcroft mused over the mixed blessing of mastery over time. One of the most important scientific discoveries of the twenty-first century had been the ability to bend time. Immediately lauded, enormous resources were invested to develop this knowledge as part of the scientific arms race. The discovery was not made in time to end the drawn-out conflicts between the political powers, but development continued under the leadership of the UNA following the acts of mutual destruction that did finally end them.

Before long, UNA scientists had discovered how to send objects, then robots, then partially human androids back in time using a number of closely guarded time-travel portals. However, initial experiments exposed the dangerous consequences of even the smallest change made in the past. Famous incidents, such as the sudden disappearance of entire extended families in 2071, gave rise to widespread political and civil unrest. Once the last pockets of protest had been extinguished, and the UNA's disinformation machine had completed its final official denial, it was decided that future exploitation of time portals should be severely limited, and top secret.

Following the destruction of the Wellington reactor in 2110, President Westcroft commissioned an investigation by a working group of trusted experts into how—hypothetically—known time portals could be used to most effectively alter the history of the world to avoid catastrophe. He made clear to the team of scientists, historians, anthropologists, futurists, mathematicians, demographers and psychologists that any attempt to interfere with history would only be made when all hope of an alternative outcome had been extinguished.

The eighteenth president of the UNA knew that time was at hand.

"There is no doubt," continued Council Secretary Lomax, "that what is left of our world is at the point of utmost need. And it is with this in mind that a vote has been taken on our next course of action. This vote is in favour of invoking Operation Reset."

A murmur spread throughout the packed room. As Secretary Lomax walked painfully to her seat, closely supported by the android, the murmur intensified. The president rose and with both palms tried to regain order.

"Ladies and gentlemen! My friends!" Westcroft said, waiting for the crowd to settle. "And so we come to the crux of the matter." He raised his eyebrows and sighed gently. "You have been presented with the facts, and now we know the result of what could well be the most important vote in the history of civilisation."

The fifty or so senior politicians, technologists, engineers and high-ranking military officers who had been summoned now sat transfixed.

Westcroft continued. "So, now we must decide the appropriate course of action."

The president paused again, glancing around the auditorium at the stern, familiar faces gazing back at him with respectful attention. He took a second or two to reflect on how several of them had formerly scowled in disagreement at his decisions; some had been fierce political opponents. Now, at last, there was a unity forged from their common purpose and shared anxieties.

"You have all been privy to top secret information on the Authority's time programme and will be aware of both its capabilities and its dangers. Indeed, some of you have firsthand knowledge of time travel operations, and those of you in the Disinformation Department have soiled your hands with the unsavoury but vitally important task of removing all traces of past time travel mishaps from recorded history and human memory.

"I do not propose to revisit past incidents, or to rekindle the passionate but earnest debates that we have had, in this very auditorium, about the moral and legal issues surrounding the decision to go back in time. There is no time for that now. Suffice it to say that every one of us is aware of the power of this weapon that we possess, and of what can go wrong once that particular genie is released from the bottle.

"Nevertheless, it will come as no surprise to any of you to learn that the Authority has been making preparations to do just that—preparing for a course of action that must only be implemented in the utmost need, in line with resolutions ratified by this council. But now we must release that genie, so it is important that we all have full knowledge of the contingency plans that have been prepared."

Westcroft turned towards a man seated to his right. Dressed in a Lincoln-green military uniform with silver buttons and a gold braiding hung loosely between the point of his right shoulder and the adjacent lapel, General Paul Steyning immediately rose, needing no further cue from the president.

A career soldier, Steyning's military background was expressed in his upright posture and his immaculately tidy grey hair, neatly parted on the left. He strutted to a transparent lectern with a brisk, business-like gait. A gesture with his right hand simultaneously dimmed the lighting in the auditorium and initiated a three-dimensional presentation space that floated just a few feet above his head. Dispensing with formalities—not even taking the time to acknowledge Westcroft, who had been his friend and ally since their early military academy days—Steyning immediately launched into a dry, factual description of the preparations that had been made for Operation Reset.

"Operation Reset," he began. "Nine years, three research departments, personnel totalling 173. A great deal of time and effort has been sacrificed in drawing up a contingency plan for a retrospective intervention. I must confess that I never thought that we would be in a position to have to implement such a plan. However, preparations have been made with great care and in great detail.

"Following our honourable president's lead, I will not hand-wring over previous bitter experience with such interventions, but you will all understand that any necessary interference in past events must be made with a surgical precision. For that reason, our teams of statistical analysts, industrial historians, and military strategists have made a very detailed study of the events that have led us to this current crisis."

The presentation began with a vivid representation of the UNA's dark-blue-and-silver logo, emblazoned with the words *TOP SECRET*.

"The conclusion to our analysis of past events is that the root of the current crises lies in the decision, in the early part of the twenty-first century, to stake all of the world's future on nuclear power. Our probability analysts have considered a number of other options and have run simulations of literally hundreds of scenarios in search of alternative solutions. We have considered changes to military outcomes, diplomatic exchanges, and events that have affected world financial markets. But no others have been able to substantially alter our fate."

As Steyning spoke, the meeting delegates, seated in a circle on all sides of the 3-D presentation space, observed a display of images synchronised with the general's recitation of key events that had shaped the world's past.

"As a military man," he continued, "it is hard for me to come to terms with the fact that, after all the lives that have been lost as a result of armed conflicts over the past 250 years, no change in the result of any individual engagement or extended campaign would have significantly altered the course of history. It appears, ladies and gentlemen, that winning and losing—an obsession of mine throughout my entire career—has been little more than a red herring in the greater scheme of things."

The 3-D presentation paused, and the display dimmed slightly as the general took a second or two to clear his throat and collect his thoughts. A quiet murmur spread throughout the auditorium. Those gathered were unused to seeing Steyning display such humility. Compared with his usual self-confidence and bullish bearing, this frank admission bordered on self-doubt.

"But we are not here to reflect on such ironies," he continued. "That's something for future historians to worry about. What we must decide is the most appropriate course of action for the current situation.

"The general conclusion of our deliberations is that, as ever, it is *people* who change the course of history. People who can lead others. People who can change the way that others think. And, fortunately, individuals can be eliminated easily, cleanly and with minimal collateral impact on events."

As he spoke, images of well-known personalities of the past filled the presentation space: President Abraham Lincoln, President

John Fitzgerald Kennedy, Martin Luther King Jr., Leon Trotsky, Diana Princess of Wales, Archduke Franz Ferdinand of Austria, Yasser Arafat al-Qudwa and a succession of others who had, over the previous two centuries, died in mysterious circumstances.

"You will all recognise before you people who have been thought leaders and global decision makers in the past. Many of these, as you all know, have been the subject of our own interventions, and even at this juncture I am not at liberty to divulge which ones, but some of these interventions have been more successful than others."

Another faint murmur rose from the gathered delegates. President Westcroft lifted the palm of his right hand to silence them.

"The point is," continued General Steyning, "that our analysis has concluded that it is not feasible to eliminate whole corporations, or whole industries to prevent the rise and domination of nuclear power—not without causing wholesale and uncontrollable collateral impacts. And so, I am about to propose a radical solution."

The presentation space filled with an image of a young man with blond hair swept back from his forehead, and who was dressed in a manner unmistakably characteristic of the early twenty-first century.

"This is Dr. Benjamin Aaron Richards," the general announced. "Born in London, Europe, on the 11th of February 1984. The son of Leonard Edward Richards, an aeronautical engineer, and Melissa Anne Jean Hammond, a schoolteacher."

The delegates gazed at the 3-D image of Ben Richards as it rotated slowly, wondering why this previously unknown young man might hold the key to the world's future. They didn't have to wait long for an explanation.

"Benjamin Richards was trained as an aeronautical engineer, like his father, but developed a specialisation in what were, at the time, fairly rudimentary wind turbines. He worked in this area in the very early years of the development of wind-power technology, from around 2010 to 2017. We are convinced that the technology he was developing, allied to his plans for siting wind turbines in city-centre locations, had the potential to roll out worldwide, and could have provided a source of clean and freely available energy in every continent."

"Then why didn't he? And why did he only work in the field for about seven years?" asked an anxious voice from the audience. "And why has nobody heard of him?" asked another.

General Steyning, surprised at this sudden and uncharacteristic breach of protocol, shot a glance at President Westcroft, who leaned forward in his chair.

"The reason that you've not heard of the unfortunate Dr. Richards," Steyning said, raising his voice, "is that the young man died suddenly, in 2017." Silence returned to the auditorium. "At the time, the cause of his death remained unexplained, and the local coroner returned an open verdict. But from what we know of the symptoms of his sudden illness, and using the knowledge that we now have, it appears that he was poisoned."

"Evidence? Motive?" snapped a voice to the general's right.

President Westcroft answered. "Well, it's very difficult to be precise with a death that occurred such a long time ago, but Richards' medical records point very strongly to him having been poisoned with polonium-210. As for a motive, and as to how the isotope found its way into his bloodstream, it's impossible to be sure," the president said. "But somebody must have had a very good reason for killing Richards. Polonium-210 was very difficult to come by in those days. It was used in small quantities in the early space programmes, when mankind had barely ventured much farther than the earth's moon. So, it could not have found its way into somebody's bloodstream by accident!

"Our proposal is to implement a variation on our usual intervention method, and actually *prevent* the death of Dr. Benjamin Richards."

Delegates muttered and guffawed. "But how can you be sure that Richards would have followed through on his ideas?" asked one. "How can you be sure of the collateral impacts of letting this man live for, say, another fifty years?" demanded another. "Yes, he might have had ten children," said a third.

The president raised both hands to silence the crowd.

"Yes, I know the risks, far better than any of you," Steyning said. "But we have considered every possible eventuality, and our analysts have calculated all the probabilities. From what we know of Richards, he was a rather solitary figure who found relationships with the opposite sex difficult, and so we estimate that there is a 70 percent probability that he would never have married and would never have had children."

Steyning's explanation was met with a rising tide of dissent, with some delegates standing. Arguments broke out between those in favour and those against. The aging president sank back in his dark-blue leather chair. He had the air not of a chairman who had lost control of a meeting, but of a judge who was now certain of a course of action and biding his time before making a final pronouncement.

President Westcroft stood. "My decision, in ratification of the vote that we have taken, is to approve the initiation of Operation Reset. We must go back to 2017 and save Dr. Benjamin Richards."

CHAPTER 3

SHUI FENG

Miles Cardus strode grim-faced down the long, broad flight of marble steps that drew the eye to the United Nations Authority's magnificent headquarters. The landmark consisted of 138 stories of silver steel and aquamarine-tinted glass mimicking the shape of a gull about to take flight. It was by no means the tallest structure in Melbourne, but it was the jewel in the city's crown, and had just hosted the most important meeting of politicians, defence chiefs and industry leaders in history.

Cardus's youthful appearance for a man of sixty-six was the product of a very close professional relationship with one of the foremost cosmetic surgeons in Australasia, and heredity. A gap between his two front teeth caused him to speak with a soft lisp, creating the initial impression of almost child-like affability. But Miles Matthew Jacobus McIntyre Cardus was no child; he was the veteran of many a boardroom battle, someone who took pride in possessing an instinctive ability to focus on the strategic assets and alliances necessary to maintain control of the industrial energy sector—in the form of GIATCOM International. Miles represented the fifth generation of the Cardus family to spearhead the colossal nuclear power conglomerate. He had also rapidly acquired a reputation for being the most ruthless negotiator around and a person who valued the life's work of his forefathers above all else.

Cardus was the first of 150 delegates to leave the meeting. With his grade-A security pass, he soon emerged from the air-conditioned main meeting hall into the sunshine of yet another stiflingly warm February afternoon. He barely noticed the extreme change of temperature, being so distracted with President Westcroft's announcement a mere ten minutes earlier.

Cardus stepped into his air-conditioned personal transport pod preset to return him to his main office in Compton Town, Melbourne's central business district. He sank back into the soft, white leather seat, but relaxation was the last thing on his mind. With a smooth, horizontal wave of his right hand, he activated the pod's communication device. After a few seconds, he was face-to-face with a three-dimensional hologram of Shui Feng Yang.

"Do you have any news for me?" Cardus blurted. "What have you been able to find out about this Dr. Benjamin Richards?"

"So far, only that he was an aeronautical engineer and a would-be, but unsuccessful, wind-energy entrepreneur. It appears that the most remarkable achievement of his life was to die. Most of what was written about him concerned the mystery of his death, given that knowledge of the poison that killed him remained a closely guarded military secret for several years after his assassination," Feng said.

Feng was a product of military research known to a select few and properly understood by even fewer. It was generally thought that the enhanced human research (EHR) programmes of the mid-twenty-first century had been abandoned in favour of investment in the development of artificial intelligence in the robotics industry, which led to the prevalence of advanced androids and drones being employed for manufacturing, law enforcement and surveillance. The truth was that the programmes were secretly financed and controlled by a consortium of businesses, of which GIATCOM was one. With control of 95 percent of the world's communications technology and media, there had been no problem hiding from the public the development of enhanced humans, especially with so much of the world's attention focused on the periodic nuclear disasters that had blighted human history.

By the early 2060s, China was by far the most advanced nation in terms of EHR, particularly in the field of military applications. In the years leading up to the Chinese government's decision to withdraw its support for research and development, its military programme was a mixture of spectacular technical and scientific advancements and an exceptionally high rate of wastage among the products. Some of the surviving units became the property of Chinese government officials who used them for various illegal and morally questionable purposes.

Shui Feng was one of a small number of individuals from the programme who had been shipped off to Australasia in return for the political asylum that the Confederation of Australasia granted some of the leading proponents of China's EHR programme. The Australian deserts represented the few remaining areas of the world where EHR could develop unnoticed and unhindered. Miles Cardus took a close personal interest in the development of the technology. He also availed himself of the services of Shui Feng in particular, and the two had developed a close personal and professional relationship.

"Well, he is certainly the target of the UNA, which means that he is now our target," continued Cardus. "I have the precise details of where and when the Authority will open the portal, and I have already transmitted these details to you." Cardus leaned forward in his seat. "You understand what it is that I need you to do?"

Feng raised his eyebrows, surprised that his longtime collaborator should ask such a question given that Cardus himself had been a leading sponsor in developing Feng's advanced intelligence and powers of reasoning.

"Yes, I understand precisely what is required of me," he said.

"My guess is that the Authority will send Agent Merisi once again, and his remit will be to prevent Richards' assassination. I don't care how you do it. Eliminate Merisi if you have to. Just make sure that you do not fail me."

"I will not let you down," said Feng with an air of certainty. "What assistance will you be able to provide?"

"The usual kit that we have used before for this type of work; no heavy weaponry, but everything that you'll need to carry out the task. I will provide you with android assistance—at least one unit, maybe two."

"Specification?" asked Feng.

"At least TX Series—better than that, if I can."

Cardus glanced out the window of his pod and saw the suburbs of Melbourne flashing past. He sighed, returning his attention to the image of Feng.

"We have three days in which to make the necessary preparations before the portal is opened, and then you will be transported to a point in time that is precisely seventy-two hours before Richards' assassination. That means that you have six days in which to learn everything you can about the target. I have sent you an image of Richards that was taken about a year before his death."

"Yes, I am sure that I will be able to find him."

"But you cannot leave a mess behind," Cardus said, concerned at Feng's fairly flippant attitude. "You need to be subtle and use all the skills you possess for blending into your environment."

"Understood!"

"That means that you might need to gain the target's confidence, so you will need to learn everything about him—his character, his preferences, his fears, his weaknesses."

"I will not fail," declared Feng.

With that, Cardus terminated the communication with the same horizontal hand gesture with which it had been initiated. Now all was silent, except for the constant whisper of wind against the pod.

CHAPTER 4

DINNER WITH A JOURNALIST

JULY 4, 2017

Ben Richards felt strangely tense, despite the posh surroundings of the lobby of Florence's Hotel Savoy and the comfort of the plush, cream sofa in which he was reclined. Was it the events of the afternoon at the Ponte Vecchio that had set him on edge? Or was it his impending interview with an Italian journalist who would surely ask penetrating questions?

Grazia Rossini, thought Richards, turning the journalist's name over and over in his head. He had no real problem with meeting people for the first time, but he had an irrational fear of forgetting the person's name. *Could be embarrassing.* As an Englishman, it was perfectly natural for him to dread embarrassment—surely the very worst of all possible outcomes. *Rossini. Typical Italian name,* he thought. *I wonder how good her English is. I don't want to have to communicate with her in sign language.*

There had not been much of a language barrier when the pair spoke on the phone a few times to discuss the article. The writer was a twenty-four-year-old in her first year on the newspaper's staff. He suspected that conversation in English might be a little more difficult for her in a social setting, once she was unable to use purely technical language.

Rossini's article was intended to feed the world's growing interest in alternative energy resources and coincided with the paper that Richards was due to present at the Instituto di Energia in Milan in two days. Her newspaper, with its largely urban circulation, was intrigued by the British aerodynamics expert's ideas for generating energy from wind turbines in city centres, especially after he had circulated a press release suggesting that football stadia might be ideal locations for such turbines.

For Rossini, it was an opportunity to meet someone whose work she had long admired. The pursuit of sustainable energy resources and the protection of the natural environment were a passion. Her childhood had been spent in a remote village some thirty miles from the southern city of Bari, and she had never been far from nature during her formative years. She turned down several opportunities for positions in the mainstream Italian press in Milan and Turin—*La Stampa, Corriere della Sera*, even *La Gazzettadello Sport*—preferring instead to focus on the subject areas that were closest to her heart.

Richards glanced at his watch. The journalist had booked dinner for them at 7:30, and they were to meet in the foyer for a drink fifteen minutes earlier, which Richards felt was the civilised way to do business. But Rossini was late!

• •

Grazia Rossini stared intently at her laptop screen. She was alone in the vast, open-plan office of *La Nazione*'s editorial headquarters in the Vialedella Giovine Italia, Florence. There were others working late in offices along the featureless, unloved corridor, but Rossini was oblivious to the occasional slamming door or the raised voice of a colleague having an animated conversation on the telephone. With her immediate coworkers all having retired to the Book Pub, a favourite journalist haunt just around the corner, Grazia was determined to be well prepared for her very important interview.

She had just finished reading Dr. Ben Richards' most recent paper on the exploitation of the Coanda Effect for maximising energy yield from roof-mounted turbines. She was searching for a similar article by Volker Boer, a Dutchman working in the same field as Richards, when she was interrupted by the shrill alarm of her mobile phone. Grazia had meticulously calculated the time that it would take her to leave the office and arrive for her meeting with Richards at the Hotel Savoy—a twenty-minute walk. The alarm reminded her to shut down her computer and leave. But there was surely value to be had from skimming just one more article.

Rossini smiled nervously at the grey-coated doorman and passed through the double doors of the hotel's main entrance ten minutes late. Struggling to maintain her grip on her notepad, pencil, phone, car keys and small handbag, she stopped and scanned the dozen or so guests loitering in the high-ceilinged foyer adorned with chandeliers, marble floors and ornate wall sconces.

Rossini had a sparrow-like figure and jet-black, bobbed hair. Her dark-brown eyes and olive skin betrayed her Southern Italian origins. She was wearing tan sandals with a slight heel, white summer slacks that extended to the top of her calves, and a loose-fitting red blouse that hinted that the wearer was lacking a little in self-confidence. Rossini did not fit the self-assured woman that Richards had imagined from her telephone manner, but there was no doubt that the small figure blinking in the intense light of the hotel's grand entrance hall was the person he was expecting, and so he rose to greet her.

As the tall, blue-suited man approached, Rossini smiled, relieved that she had come to the right hotel, albeit a tad late.

"Dr. Richards?" she said, proffering her hand after hurriedly tucking notepad, phone and other paraphernalia under her left arm.

"You must be Grazia Rossini," Richards said.

"Thank you for agreeing to see me," she replied. "As I said on the phone, my editor wants to run a story about your innovations."

"Well, that's a conversation best held over dinner, wouldn't you agree?"

"I do, especially since my paper is paying."

Richards led the journalist straight into the hotel's spacious restaurant. They walked through a wide corridor festooned with oil reproductions of Caravaggio masterpieces. Richards only gave these a cursory glance as he was intrigued by the waif-like figure following half a pace behind. Rossini's expensive aroma seemed at odds with the brisk, child-like flapping of her sandals on the polished marble floor.

Moments later, they were being seated in richly-upholstered chairs with slender, curved wooden arms.

"Dry martini," Rossini said as a waiter arrived.

"What a coincidence!" Richards said.

"What do you mean?"

"That's my favourite aperitif."

"Well, make it two, then." She smiled to the waiter.

Richards studied the laughter lines around Rossini's eyes and was delighted by a dimple in her left cheek.

"So, please tell me about these turbines of yours," Rossini said, placing her notepad and phone on the table. She felt a little nervous at being with a man several years her senior, but her strictly professional facade would dispel any romantic notions he might have.

Her no-nonsense approach made Richards feel more at ease as he was not used to female company, largely due to always giving his work priority. Nevertheless, he felt rather warm under the collar. He undid the top button of his shirt and loosened his tie, avoiding contact with Rossini's large brown eyes.

"Ah! My wind turbines," he began. Richards told Rossini about his ideas for the sustainable generation of energy using wind turbines in urban areas. It was a succinct summary that did not differ greatly from the abstract to his conference paper that he was in Italy to deliver. He found solace in the familiar subject area. Rossini listened attentively, studying Richards' face. She wore the hint of a smile, which helped Richards to relax and encouraged him to speak freely about his work.

"Are you all prepared for your keynote presentation?" she asked.

"Yes, I suppose so."

"Ready to give a sparkling performance, no doubt?"

"Well, I hope so."

Rossini was surprised at the experienced engineer's tepid response. She wondered if it was uncertainty or humility.

"You must have made many presentations before—haven't you?" she asked.

"True," replied Richards. "But you never quite know how things are going to turn out until you actually walk on that stage." As he spoke, memories of feeling nervous on stage as a schoolboy flooded his mind. He had very much been the nerd of his class and was consistently bullied as a child. Despite the quite impressive physique he developed as an adult, he had been a short and weedy youth, not growing to his full height until his late teens.

"Are you ready to order?" The voice of the waiter, who had approached them unnoticed, dragged Richards from his reminiscence. The waiter placed the martinis on the table, and the pair turned their attention to the brown, leather-clad menus. Rossini took just a few seconds to decide.

"I'll start with *antipasti misto*," she said. "Then *chianina* steak, medium rare, with a glass of house Chianti."

"And for you, sir?"

"Same," said Richards as he took his martini glass in one hand, spilling a little due to a slight tremor in his hand, a subconscious nervous reaction to being awoken from a reverie or a cocoon of intense concentration.

"Are you okay, Dr. Richards? You seem a little shaken."

"But not stirred," Richards quickly replied as he struggled to find a smile.

"Not to worry, sir. I will clean it up," said the waiter as he dabbed at the spillage with the cloth that had been draped over his arm. "Any *contorni* potatoes?"

"Not for me," Grazia said.

Richards shook his head. The waiter bowed slightly and left.

"Now then, Dr. Richards, tell me why you've come all the way to Italy."

Rossini took a sip before placing her drink back on the table and taking hold of her pencil.

"As I was saying, I'm going to Milan to speak about a new technology that has the capacity to save the planet."

"That's a grand claim," she said, looking up from her pad.

"It is, but I believe it."

"You believe it? That sounds like the language of religion."

"Maybe *believe* is the wrong word," Richards said.

"Perhaps you know the old saying," Rossini said.

"Which one?"

"About beliefs and convictions."

"I don't know it, no."

"In your language it sounds better. It goes like this. A belief is something you hold. A conviction is something that holds you."

"Yes!" Richards exclaimed. "That's it exactly—a conviction. I am not a believer. At least not in a religious sense."

Rossini chuckled. "So, your belief is based on your own findings? A passionate scientist!" she cried. "That is a contradiction. I'm dying to hear what it is that has captivated you so."

"It all boils down to this," Richards said. "The resources in our planet are not a bottomless pit. They will run out, and perhaps sooner than we realise."

"Tell me more," Grazia said as she folded open a new page on her notebook.

"Well, as a reporter you will have heard the news recently that in my country, the UK, the spare capacity for energy generation has reduced from 17.5 percent five years ago to just 5 percent a year ago."

"I wrote about it in my newspaper," Rossini said.

"Then you'll know that this year it's gone down to 4.1 percent and that we are running out of power for the UK's commercial and domestic energy markets."

"I do."

"And you'll also know that the alternative solutions, such as offshore and onshore greenfield wind farming, are not just an eyesore. They are ironically also harmful to the environment."

Richards paused as the waiter returned with two large oval plates covered with cured meats. As soon as he had gone, Richards finished his cocktail and took a bite of the antipasti. He looked up and stared into Rossini's eyes as the flame of the guttering candle burned in the centre of her dark pupils.

"I work as a research scientist within the wind energy industry," Richards continued. "And I've been trying to encourage a completely new way of thinking about energy generation."

"A paradigm shift?" the young journalist asked.

"Precisely. I am convinced that there is a way forward, but it involves us employing a different approach from anything we've done before."

"What exactly?"

"My idea is to build roof-mounted turbine arrays on top of urban buildings."

"What kind of buildings?"

"Well, the ideal ones in most of our cities are football stadiums. Turbines built on these would not mar the landscape, harm the environment or cost as much as those built in greenfield sites. They'd not only generate enough power for the needs of the stadium but for their community too. After all, most football stadiums only need to consume energy two or three days each week."

Grazia leaned forward. "Does this technology work?"

"My tests show that it does."

"But what about prototypes on actual stadiums? Have you built any yet?"

Richards sighed and took a sip of wine. "That's my main problem. The recession has made people nervous about investing in pilot schemes like mine. So I have no examples to cite as best practice as yet."

"So, it's not just energy that's running out," Grazia said. "It's money too."

"And leaders as well. For this to transition from dream to reality, I am going to need compelling leaders, both governmental and industry ones. Without great leadership, this will never get off the ground."

"You have many challenges, Dr. Richards."

"Then there's the threat of the new," Richards said.

"What do you mean?"

"I mean that there are people who will stop at nothing to protect the old technologies, especially if it's lining their pockets.

And they'll stop at nothing to prevent the new technologies from displacing them."

"Are you saying that you're in danger?" Rossini asked, lowering her voice and leaning forward.

Richards paused and glanced around the restaurant. The only person within earshot was a plump, sweating man sipping wine alone at the table behind him.

Richards leaned into the light emanating from the candle flame.

"I think someone may have tried to stun, maybe even kill me this afternoon," he whispered.

"How do you know?"

"Look at this."

Richards drew a handkerchief from his pocket and unfolded it. There in the centre lay the red-tailed dart.

"This was shot from a high-powered rifle. It would have hit me in the face had not a stranger raised my camera to protect me."

"A stranger?" Grazia asked as she took the dart and examined it. "Describe him."

"He had jet-black hair, your colour, and a goatee. And he wore a white, three-piece suit."

Grazia's eyes dilated as she returned the dart.

"Are you sure?"

"Yes, do you know him?"

"There was someone answering that description in the foyer of the hotel when I arrived."

"Do you think it might be the same man? Am I being watched?"

"It seems you may be," Rossini replied.

"But who would want to shoot me?" Richards asked, peering around the restaurant once again. "And why would a complete stranger come to my aid like that?"

"Maybe your innovations are attracting attention from, let's say, beyond your realm of vision."

"All I'm trying to do is save the world from running out of energy."

"I'm afraid prophets have a very low life expectancy," she sighed.

The waiter arrived with their steaks and salad.

Rossini raised her Chianti. "Here's to a perfect Tuscan marriage, Dr. Richards."

After a small mouthful of steak, Rossini put her notebook into her leather messenger bag and withdrew her cell phone. She sent a text. Within seconds, the phone vibrated loudly on the table, and Grazia glanced at the illuminated screen.

"Good," she said.

"What?"

"That was my editor. He's given me permission to cover the whole of the seminar and the buildup to it."

"Are you sure that's necessary?"

"Dr. Richards, the upcoming seminar is an extremely important one, and our newspaper has a great deal of interest in it. And your ideas could be central to the whole agenda. We might as well travel together. While you finish your steak, I'm going to reception to book myself—if you don't mind, of course."

It was an unusual situation for Richards to find himself in, but he saw no objection and so shrugged slightly, which he hoped Rossini would not mistake for indifference. She rose and took her bag. As she walked away, Richards looked at the young woman not as an object of desire but as an astute potential colleague and ally.

After several minutes, Rossini returned, bent low over Richards, and said in a hushed voice, "Do not be under any illusions, Dr. Richards. Your ideas are not just sound; they are critical. It is life and death for planet earth."

She leaned even closer so that she was now whispering in Richards' ear. "If you succeed in carrying them out, in one hundred years your name will be revered by everyone alive on this dying planet."

Richards looked into her eyes.

"I pray for you," she said.

CHAPTER 5

CHANCE MEETING

Richards was so engrossed in thought about his extraordinary day once Grazia left to make her plans that he hardly noticed the quality of his meal. *How could one so young be so sure of such a thing? Do I really have what it takes to save a dying planet?*

As he placed his knife and fork on his empty plate, Richards became aware of a man approaching. He assumed that it was the waiter, but it was the portly, middle-aged gentleman who had been sitting at the table behind him.

"Forgive me for interrupting your meal," said the man, who had patiently waited for Richards to finish his main course. "I would be grateful for a moment of your time."

"Yes, of course," said Richards with a puzzled look. "What can I do for you?"

"Let me introduce myself," the man said. "My name is Tony Clarke, and I am chairman of Norwich City Football Club. If you follow football, you'll know that we've just been promoted to the Premier League."

"The Canaries!" exclaimed Richards, demonstrating that he had some knowledge of the beautiful game.

"Precisely! I am actually here in Italy for a few days to look at a couple of players that we might take on loan next season."

He drew back the seat that Rossini had vacated and got to the point. "Now, you're going to think me very rude, but I couldn't help overhearing what you were saying to your delightful companion earlier. I caught the phrases *wind turbines* and *football stadiums.*"

"Yes, that's right."

"Then I would really like to discuss this with you. You see, we are looking to expand our stadium, and also to upgrade our facilities so that we can be of greater service to our city. We want to take our capacity from 27,000 to 40,000, ideally before the season after next. This will mean building a new upper tier of seating right the way around the stadium, and therefore a completely new roof."

Richards warmed to his new acquaintance as a smile broke out across Clarke's rosy face.

"So, you see, there may be serendipity in my eavesdropping."

"Yes, I can see that," said Richards. "Can I get the waiter to fetch you a drink, Mr. Clarke?" He looked around the sparsely populated room for the man who had served him earlier.

"Don't mind if I do . . . and please call me Tony."

"Ben . . . Ben Richards," said the engineer as he extended his hand to Clarke.

An alert, white-jacketed waiter hurried to the table.

"What would you like, Tony?"

"Mine's a scotch with just a splash."

"So that will be two whiskeys; doubles. I'll have ice with mine."

The waiter strutted off briskly.

"So," began Clarke. "Tell me why football stadiums are the perfect place for wind turbines."

"The short answer is because they only operate at full capacity on match days, which probably means two to three days out of every seven."

"How does that help us?"

"Well, that depends on whether you are really serious about adding benefit and value to the community—not just to yourselves."

"Explain."

"Most boards of professional football clubs would only consider putting solar PV on about a quarter of their stadium roof space. That would give them enough power for their own needs, giving them a large saving on energy costs, but nothing for their neighbours."

"What are you suggesting then?"

"I am suggesting covering some of the roof space with a carefully installed array of wind turbines to generate as much renewable energy as possible."

"How would that benefit my club?" Clarke asked.

"In at least three ways. First, you would make huge savings on your own energy bills. Second, you'd not only generate enough power for your own needs but also the community. Third, you'd be making a visible and laudable stand against fuel poverty."

"Fuel poverty?"

"Our reserves are running out, at least as far as our traditional sources of energy are concerned. We are quite literally becoming bankrupt in terms of fuel."

Richards paused as the waiter returned with their order.

"The situation is grave," he continued. "Much of our fuel comes from nonrenewable sources. Our supplies of oil will run out in fifty years, natural gas in seventy years, coal in a couple hundred years."

Clarke splashed water into his scotch and raised the glass. "Cheers!" he said. He took a sip and asked, "What about nuclear power?"

"Reactors are incredibly expensive to run, and the waste produced by them is extremely toxic and needs to be stored for hundreds of thousands of years. And let's not forget the devastating effects on the environment and local communities when there are accidents."

"Chernobyl, Fukushima," pondered Clarke.

"Exactly!" Richards said. "Wind is a potentially infinite source of energy. There are no negative consequences in terms of greenhouse gases and, installed on the right structures in urban contexts, they will not mar the landscape at all."

"I see," Clarke said, wiping a bead of sweat from his brow.

"Imagine if Norwich City Football Club were the first to pioneer renewable power generation for its city. Think of the plaudits, both nationally and locally. And consider the domino effect."

"Yes. We start, and other clubs follow," Clarke mused.

"Precisely. Norwich City would be the first of the early adopters."

Clarke chuckled. "You make a good pitch, Ben, but let me ask you another question. Are there any engineering challenges? I mean, what about the vibrations caused by the turbines? Won't these cause damage to the stadium roof?"

"Not if the roof is designed properly and the turbines are installed correctly. You have the opportunity right now to design a roof that can absorb the vibrations from the turbines."

"How?"

"You'd use a truss, cantilever system for your roofing structure, rather than the cable-and-mast approach. Plus, we'd install special dampers."

"Do you have any existing structures we could look at?" Clarke asked.

"I'm afraid the economic recession has so far prevented that."

"Well, we're coming out of that," Clarke said as he drained his glass.

"Which is why there's a window open right now for someone like you to exercise leadership and make your football stadium the first in the country to provide renewable energy for their city, not just themselves."

"It's a huge investment," Clarke sighed. "Who would pay it?"

"My economic innovation stems from a football club saving on energy costs but also making money besides revenue through football. It's about becoming an energy provider as a micro grid within an urban environment, making best use of its building structure and maximising the stadium's full operational potential. This would save clubs from going into liquidation and having to sell off their best players, as they will have a second stream of income revenue from selling the electricity the stadium doesn't use.

"My estimate is a 70 percent saving. On match days, a typical football club might use all the energy generated, but generally, this is probably two days per week. On the other five days, the electricity generated from the turbines can be sold back to the grid to be used by the local community. So, it's in a football club's best interest to raise the capital investment for the turbine array themselves so that they make money from selling the electricity they generate."

"That won't happen, Ben. We are on the verge of financial ruin already—not a chance in raising funds to invest in such a fantastical venture!"

"The best idea is to subsidise the capital investment in the roof-mounted turbines from an apportioned amount of fans' ticket sales—say, 20 percent to pay for greener energy."

Clarke looked at Richards, sighed, then shook his head.

"You could of course increase ticket prices to account for the 20 percent being paid for the greener energy. In return, the local fans will be using the electricity generated at a lower price. The energy will be directed to their energy account and will make them and the club more socially responsible, improving their carbon footprint and helping to reduce carbon emissions. This will be excellent PR for you and might attract more investment in your club from private and corporate investors wanting to invest in an ethical business model."

"Yes, it all sounds very fancy, Ben, but this is unknown territory for us."

"Fortune favours the brave; isn't that what they say, Tony?"

Clarke nodded.

"These are just options that I have considered," continued Richards, "but they are quite feasible, if you do the maths. Don't forget that your club will have the extra TV money as a result of being in the Premier League next year, which could be ring-fenced for precisely such a community-focused initiative."

"It's still a risk," Clarke said.

"True," Richards said. "But there is something that might be even more feasible."

"Which is?"

"There is always a high chance of you engaging a wealthy private investor who would be happy to invest in your club."

Clarke slowly raised an eyebrow at the thought.

"In my experience, there are two types of leaders," Richards continued. "There are *risk-takers* and there are *undertakers*. Risk-takers lead people into new ventures that bring life and purpose. And undertakers . . ."

Clarke chuckled. "Bravo, Ben."

"Don't oversee initiatives that contribute to the death of our planet," Richards concluded. "Embrace ones that give it life!"

Clarke looked into Richards' eyes and studied them. He then withdrew a silver card case from the trouser pocket of his creased, grey suit.

"These are my contact details," he said.

Richards reached into a back pocket and pulled out a small wallet. "Here are mine. Contact me anytime." He then opened a thin, leather-bound folder beside him on the table and produced a glossy brochure with the title *RUACH PROJECT* emblazoned in gold on the cover.

"You'll need this for your next board meeting," he said, smiling.

Clarke took the brochure into his plump, sweaty hand. "What does *Ruach* mean?"

"It's the Hebrew word for wind. It can also mean breath . . . and spirit."

"Interesting!"

"I chose it because the project is about harnessing the wind, and also because one day we won't be able to breathe if we go on as we are. And, finally, because it will take someone of unusual spirit to lead us into this new era of renewable energy." Richards reached out his hand and stared into Clarke's bloodshot eyes. "I believe you're the man," Richards said.

Clarke stood and robustly shook Richards' hand.

"One more thing, Tony."

"Yes?"

"One hundred years ago, miners in the UK took caged canaries down into the depths of the pits. When toxic gases were present, the canaries would pass out, warning the miners to get out."

"My grandfather was a miner," Clarke interrupted. "He used to tell me stories about how lives were saved by those brave birds."

"Wouldn't it be poignant," Richards said, "if your Canaries saved lives today and in the future?"

Clarke's eyes widened.

"Good night, Tony."

With that, Tony Clarke shambled out of the restaurant, the brochure tucked under his arm.

• •

Ben Richards left the restaurant around eleven and crossed the marble floor of the Hotel Savoy's entrance hall. As he waited for the lift to his fourth-floor room, he felt fatigued yet pleasantly drowsy thanks to the combined effect of the wine and the whiskey. Richards wearily wandered down the hall and into the spacious interior of his suite.

As soon as Richards closed the doors, a bearded man in a white, three-piece suit stepped from behind a marble statue on the other side of the hall. Agent Merisi spoke softly into a communication device, which he held close to his lips.

"The target has now retired to his room . . . He wasn't followed . . . Yes, I know . . . It will take me less than twenty minutes to get to the centre of the city, to intercept them."

He stowed the device away in his waistcoat pocket and slipped out of the hotel.

CHAPTER 6

NIGHT IN FLORENCE

As fireworks exploded in the night sky, Merisi pushed through a crowd of Bacchanalian tourists processing down a lane in the Oltrarno district of Florence. His eyes were trained ahead, locked onto two men with slick, greased-back hair and silvery grey suits that shimmered in the light of the streets. Both men stealthily moved through the ranks of revellers, shimmying one way and then another with the dexterity of a *galáctico*.

"Here, watch where you're going!" a man dressed as a mummer barked.

"*Scusi*," Merisi muttered as he weaved between two men dressed as harlequins.

A few heartbeats later, the man in the white suit watched as the men he was following swerved without warning away from the festive crowd and dived down a side street about thirty metres ahead.

Merisi swiftly made his way through a group of dawdlers and hugged the facades of artisans' studios and hole-in-the-wall wine bars until he reached the entrance of the alley they had entered. There were only shadows as he peered down the slim stone corridor.

Ducking behind a small skip full of rotting refuse, he knelt and reached inside his waistcoat. He withdrew a silver button no larger than a Florentine florin, encased in a black enamel circle. He pressed it, and instantly his white suit changed colours, moving from white to grey, then grey to dark blue, before finally morphing to pitch black.

As soon as the suit was as inky as his surroundings, the man stood. He withdrew a pair of round, black-rimmed sunglasses from a case in the inside jacket pocket, touched a discrete switch on the thick black bridge of the glasses, and pulled the ear pads out a millimetre from their temples. As he placed the glasses over his eyes, the lenses immediately came to life, revealing digital red numerals and letters on each side, which relayed data about his surroundings. The temple tips over his ears sprang to life at the same time, turning the sounds and vibrations all around from silent to audible, interpreting them for him in brief phrases through a miniscule transmitter.

The man in the black suit moved down the alleyway, his ears trained to the nuances of the night, his eyes focused on the shapes ahead. About fifteen metres into the street he paused as he heard a scurrying sound.

"Rat," the temple tips said.

A moment later there was a piercing meow.

"Cat," the voice said. The lenses revealed two shapes highlighted in infrared by their body heat. The cat had clearly caught the rat and was now digging its claws and teeth into the squealing creature's neck.

A moment later the red-and-golden glow at the centre of the rodent's outline began to fade until its heart, now a phosphorescent blue, stopped beating. The black-clad observer gazed wide-eyed as the cat hurried off into the night, carrying the lifeless trophy in its jaws.

The invisible Merisi now turned his attention back towards his own quarry. As he trained his lenses on the thick darkness ahead of him, he pushed the pads of his glasses into his nose. He felt the pad arms click, and the digital readout at the top of his darkened right lens changed from the word *Humanoid* to

Android.

In an instant the shapes of two men appeared in the geometric centre of the datum line of his lenses. According to the data being transmitted, they were exactly forty metres ahead—and they were hostiles. A moment later the lenses began to flash *Caution, Caution* in blood-red letters.

A new word appeared beneath.

Assassins.

Merisi reached into the right-hand inside pocket of his jacket and withdrew a length of wire with small silver handles at each end. He furtively moved forwards, navigating around a fallen bin and a supermarket trolley tipped on its side. When he was only twenty metres away from the two men, he hid in a damp alcove. His earpieces picked up every word of the two stalkers.

"GIATCOM, do you read?" the android on the right said into a microphone embedded in his sleeve.

The two men waited.

"GIATCOM, do you read?' he repeated.

"I read," a male voice replied. "What's your status?"

"We have located the target," the android replied. "What are your orders?"

"Where is he?"

"His current location is the Savoy Hotel. How do you want us to proceed?"

There was a pause.

"Gamma 5, you get back here," the voice crackled. "I have another mission for you."

"Logged," Gamma 5 replied.

"Gamma 4, capture the target. Take him alive. Do not, I repeat, do not let any harm come to him."

"Logged," the second android said.

With that, Gamma 5 stepped towards the wall at the end of the alley.

"Ready," he said.

The second android stepped back. As soon as he did, Gamma 5 disappeared. Gamma 4 looked to his right and left, then turned. He walked swiftly down the street.

As he passed the alcove, his pursuer sprang out and drew the garrotting wire to its full length. In less than a second, Merisi was right behind his prey, tugging the wire taut around the android's gasping throat. The victim desperately grabbed at the wire with his fingers, emitting a shrill from his tightening windpipe.

Merisi pressed switches on the small silver handles at each end of the wire, which now turned white hot, burning the skin on the android's neck.

A thin red line appeared at the nape. The smell of burning flesh filled the hunter's nostrils as the wire seared into his prey, severing flesh from all angles simultaneously, until the head parted from the neck and dropped to the ground.

The killer, poised above the android's torso, watched as the wires in the stump of the victim's neck fired briefly. The android's mouth opened.

"Pater—" he rasped. "Pater—"

Then the remaining glimmer of light went out in his eyes.

Merisi ran back to the wall at the end of the alley, taking less care this time as he jumped over and pushed through the detritus of the deserted corridor. He halted at the site where the other android had disappeared and withdrew a silver cigarette lighter from his waistcoat pocket. He lifted one side to his mouth and pressed a button at the base of the lighter.

"Come in," he said.

"UNA," a female voice replied.

"I have located the portal they've been using in Florence," Merisi said. "It's ours."

"Damn them!" the voice cried.

"And I've dispatched one of the two assassins that have been using it."

"What about the other one?"

"He returned to GIATCOM before I could finish him."

"That's unfortunate."

"What do you want me to do?"

"Neutralise the portal."

"Is that all?"

"No, continue to keep your eyes on the target and keep sending intelligence back to me."

"What about the other assassin? He's bound to return when

his accomplice doesn't report in."

"Watch over the Uffizi portal. That's the only one he can use now. If he makes an appearance, you know what to do."

The woman paused.

"The future of our planet depends on you," she added.

"I won't fail," Merisi said.

"You had better not."

Merisi put the lighter back in his pocket and pulled out an implement shaped like a large silver pen that had been attached to his belt. He stepped a few metres away from the ground where the android had disappeared and directed the pointed end towards it. He swivelled the casing at the base of the instrument, and a blue beam flowed in a perfect and uninterrupted line from the tip.

Merisi methodically traced the outline of the portal with the ray until the square was illuminated.

The lettering, formerly invisible to the naked eye, now appeared, revealing a sator square.

S	A	T	O	R
A	R	E	P	O
T	E	N	E	T
O	P	E	R	A
R	O	T	A	S

Merisi pressed the base of the implement once again. The beam doubled in size and intensity, and the letters and lines on the square began to fade until the ground was clear and the portal was closed.

He walked back to the remains of the other android and directed the rays of his eraser at the head first, then the body. Within two heartbeats all trace of the assassin had been removed.

The man placed the instrument back in his belt and retrieved the silver button from his waistcoat. He pressed it until his suit colour changed white.

He caressed his goatee for a moment before removing his round, retro sunglasses. Marching down the alleyway, he reached the warm glow and the jovial sounds in the street. The Festival of Folly was still in full swing, and the street bustled with cheering revellers.

Taking the arm of a young and pretty Italian woman, the man in the white suit danced back into the light before breaking from a tight embrace and running into the night.

CHAPTER 7

THE PONTE VECCHIO

It was midnight when Merisi broke into the Uffizi gallery using an ancient door known only to a few and a cast-iron key he had possessed for more than 400 years. Heading for the foyer, he hid in the shadows to avoid a guard patrolling the ground floor.

Passing the gallery bookstore, he swiftly climbed the grand sixteenth-century staircase to the first floor. He marched silently past marble statues of gods and men carved in the classical style, and the gilded Gothic medieval altarpieces depicting scenes from the life and death of Christ. He paused only once, at the entrance of Hall 90, a chamber containing three early masterpieces by Caravaggio. Stepping briefly inside the half-lit space, he gazed into the eyes of the Medusa, the Gorgon whose severed head was painted on a convex shield. Her mane was composed of writhing snakes and her gaping mouth filled with teeth as sharp as needles. Staring at her reflexion for the first and last time, the owner of this repulsive severed head seemed fixed forever in the horror of who she truly was. Merisi stared at the thick jets of blood shooting from the Gorgon's neck and frowned.

"Flee," he muttered, "for if your eyes are petrified in amazement, she will turn you to stone."

Snapping out of his introspection, Merisi turned and left the room. He walked away from the Palazzo Vecchio in a southerly direction towards the River Arno, pausing before an unassuming door that concealed a world to which few had access.

He reached for another key from his pocket and pushed it gently into the lock. He opened the door quietly, stepped inside and closed it behind him. Fetching his black-rimmed sunglasses from his jacket pocket, he switched the lenses into night mode.

In front of him was a long and spacious corridor stretching the full length of the Ponte Vecchio. It had been commissioned by Giorgio Vasari in 1564 at the orders of Cosimo de Medici. Originally built as a gift to his daughter Francesca on the occasion of her marriage to Giovanni of Austria, it quickly become a causeway for the Medici family whenever they wanted to cross from their political residence—the Palazzo Vecchio—to their private residence—the Palazzo Pitti—to avoid mingling with the common people.

Florence had been a dangerous city in the second half of the sixteenth century. There were frequent duels and brawls, so the raised corridor on top of the bridge afforded safe passage, and also provided an unrivalled view of Florence for the city's elite. The Medicis and their opulent friends often made their way from the Uffizi, originally constructed as administrative offices, to their private home and the famed Boboli Gardens on the other side of the river, a journey of about one kilometre. En route, they would stop and look through small circular windows at those making their way along the river or walking the streets.

The man in the white suit looked down the Corridoio Vasariano, taking in the silence, gasping as he had so many times before, and smiling at the hundreds of paintings from the seventeenth and eighteenth centuries that adorned the walls. Many of them were self-portraits by some of the greatest Italian painters. This was a silent museum reserved only for the few—another dimension altogether—lying behind an unmarked door.

Merisi stopped only to look at the scars that remained from the bombing perpetrated by the Italian Mafia in 1993. On the night of May 26, a car laden with explosives had been driven to the Torre dei Polici. When the explosives detonated, five people were killed, and a section of the Vasari Corridor was severely damaged. Several artworks had been almost obliterated. Later they were lovingly pieced back together and had taken their place again among the undamaged masterpieces, their imperfection a constant reminder of the carnage and chaos.

Merisi moved on past statues and windows, glancing unnoticed at the remaining revellers below still swinging and singing into the small hours. Having crossed over the Arno, he stopped at a grate. Past it was a small stone balcony overlooking the nave of an ancient church dedicated to Santa Felicita. The balcony, which had been built into the church's facade, was now home to several kneelers made of cedar, copies of those at which the grand dukes of the Medici family had prayed while at Mass— without, of course, mingling with the commoners below.

Merisi withdrew the pen-shaped instrument from his belt and used it to detach four metal clips fastening the left side of the grate to the wall. In an instant, the grating loosened, and he slipped onto the balcony and stood behind one of the kneelers. He looked down into the darkness of the nave and then across the marble floor towards the high altar. He fixed his attention on the floor in front of an oak door on the left of the church. Instantly, his sunglasses transmitted the data.

Uffizi Portal, it read. *Square intact.*

Merisi pulled a pistol from a concealed holster under his jacket. This was no ordinary weapon. It was designed like an early-seventeenth-century flintlock pistol made in Lombardy. The metal was ornately decorated in the Renaissance style and the frame made of wood. The grip was octagonal and adorned with golden-coloured, cast-metal decorations. The intricate barrel, trigger and striker were all fashioned from the same metal. The whole piece was designed as the weapon of choice for a nobleman. His was a replica.

Merisi turned it sideways. Flicking a tiny switch just in front of the trigger ratchet, the right-hand side of the wooden frame underneath the barrel opened to reveal a compartment that ran the full twelve inches from the hammer and flintlock to the end of the barrel.

He fed the silver pen into the chamber before closing the frame of the pistol. He then sank onto the purple cushion of the kneeler and rested the pistol over his left forearm.

Pistol and optics synchronised, the data field in his glasses revealed. The time, according to the same feed, was 0217.

Merisi kept his eyes fixed upon the floor in front of the vestry door for an hour and a half. There was no movement, no sound at all in the nave. The corridor behind him was unguarded. There were no footsteps in front or behind, no signs of life. The eyes that stared at him from almost every angle were dead, frozen in time by sculptors and painters who themselves had disappeared long ago into the dust of the earth.

Then, the data field ignited, and red-lettered words fired up on the display.

Portal activating. Ingress imminent. Illegal access.

Merisi raised his replica flintlock and gazed through his glasses down the barrel. The display immediately changed from *Data* to *Attack* mode. Instead of digits and letters, there was now a large red circle hugging the circumference of his vision, with a red dot in the epicentre. His sunglasses had turned into a tactical scope. He manoeuvred his pistol and trained the red dot on the door just in front of the chancel. As he waited, an aural feed activated, and a countdown filled his ears.

"Ten, nine, eight . . ."

Merisi slowed his breathing.

"Five, four . . ."

He held his breath.

"Two, one."

As the countdown reached zero, a phosphorescent glow appeared on the marble floor just in front of the wooden door. The illuminated shape of a man appeared in the centre of the scope. He was wearing a suit as silvery as the moon above the city.

Assassin, the lenses flashed.

As the interloper took a step, Merisi pulled the trigger. A perfect, straight line of searing energy shot from the barrel tip of the flintlock and struck the left side of the man's groin. Everything from his left knee to his lower left abdomen disappeared before he realised what had happened.

Flailing forward, the man sought desperately for some way to pull himself towards cover. But there was nothing within reach.

Startled, he looked up to the balcony, then back towards the door.

As his killer aimed once again, the android groped at the door, his mouth opened wide.

"Pat!" he cried. "No!"

The beam hit him directly in the head and then travelled down the length of his twitching body until he disappeared.

"It's done," Merisi said into the silver lighter. "The second GIATCOM assassin is terminated."

"I'm afraid you're not finished," a woman replied.

"What now?"

"We have received intelligence," the voice replied. "GIATCOM has sent someone else."

"Who?"

"Shui Feng."

The man raised his eyebrows.

"Listen, Merisi," the woman said. "It's one thing disposing of androids, but Shui Feng is the most lethal agent GIATCOM has."

"Yes, I know Feng from old. He is highly developed, just like me," Merisi said, "but unlike me, he is no more than a machine. That means he has limitations. I look forward to meeting him again."

"Be careful. Feng has never been beaten. No one has ever got close to killing him."

"Until now," Merisi said.

"Do not be so sure of yourself," the woman urged. "You may not have lost a fight in hundreds of years, but that doesn't mean you're invincible. Your scar should tell you that."

Merisi lifted a hand to the left side of his face. He could still trace the outline of a *V* after all these years. It ran from the base of his left eye to the top of his neck and had been inflicted by a dagger.

"I was beaten by three men," he said.

"I am aware of that," the woman said. "But Shui Feng is worth at least three men."

"Maybe, but I can still take him."

"Perhaps you will, but not in Florence. Our intelligence sources tell us that Feng is due to arrive in 2017 in about three hours. It is pretty certain that he will use the Siena portal; that has been GIATCOM's route in the past."

"Perfect! Then I will be waiting for him! Do we know anything about the objective of Feng's mission?"

"Not yet, but you can be certain that GIATCOM has not sent someone like Feng to merely observe. I think it's safe to assume that he will be focused on preventing you from succeeding in *your* mission."

"And if I know Feng, he will have more up his sleeve than that. For a machine, he is very unpredictable. He is not like a TX-series android, which can be programmed to behave in a precise manner. The AI he possesses enables him to improvise and to make decisions based on what he sees, hears and feels. Who knows what he will do once he gets here? He will be especially unpredictable if we don't have intelligence on his mission aims. And he is already especially unpredictable since he doesn't have morality."

"What do you mean by that?" the woman asked.

"Well, like energy, artificial intelligence is capable of being used for good or evil. Morality matters. So, making better humans with implanted artificial intelligence will always be more important than making smarter machines. Now, artificial intelligence is incapable of developing morality through cognition—"

The woman cut him off. "Just stick to the plan, Merisi, and find out what you can on him, whilst focusing on protecting Dr. Richards," she snapped.

"Of course, I could always *ask* him what his intentions are!" huffed Merisi.

"You will keep your eyes on *your* primary objective, which is to follow your target!"

"But Richards does not leave for Milan until tomorrow," said Merisi. "I can take care of Feng while my target sleeps. How far is the Siena portal from here?"

"It should not take you much more than an hour to get there, but you are not, under any circumstances, to take on Shui Feng alone. I know how much you want to defeat him, but you are far too valuable to the mission to be risked. Do you understand?"

"Well, I understand when somebody is giving me an order. I will see what happens at the Siena portal in three hours. I need to know what I'm up against on this mission—and I will report back."

"Very well. But stay out of sight. I don't suppose that any of our plans have been kept a secret from GIATCOM, but let's at least not let Feng know of your whereabouts. When was the last time you had some sleep?"

"Probably over twenty-four hours ago."

"In that case, make sure that you have some recovery time before you set off. Then take the fastest car that you can find, and remember, Feng will be looking for you."

"I saw a nice silver Lamborghini Veneno in the hotel car park earlier. Twenty-first-century cars are not difficult to get into, so that should do fine. It'll take me forty-five minutes to get to Siena."

"Well, I hope that whatever contraption you use isn't too conspicuous. Be careful not to draw attention to yourself."

Merisi smiled. "Of course."

"Seal up the Uffizi portal, and keep me informed."

"*Affirmativa*," Merisi concluded, putting the lighter back in his pocket.

Before holstering his weapon, he removed the pen-shaped object, sealed the portal and exited the balcony, reattaching the grating before he left.

Heading south, he hurried to another simple unmarked door and unlocked it. As he exited, he passed a limestone grotto filled with abstract carvings of men and beasts. Their ugly forms were illuminated by the light of the moon shining through an oculus in the centre of the frescoed ceiling.

Merisi moved swiftly past the grotto and a statue of a naked Cosimo de Medici in Bacchanalian posture. His belly was enormous as he sat on a large turtle whose shell strained beneath his weight.

Merisi chuckled, as he had a thousand times before. He then marched into the impeccably manicured gardens leading up Boboli hill behind the Palazzo Pitti. Straight away, his nostrils were filled with the scent of pink roses and juniper trees.

He approached the back of the imposing palace with its harsh, rusticated stonework. Originally the residence of a wealthy banker called Pitti, the portly Cosimo had bought it in 1549 and turned it into his family's private home, filling it over subsequent years with the finest examples of Italian art. Cosimo doubled its size as well as his weight, enlisting the help of Giorgio Vasari to build enormous extensions and the corridor that led over the Ponte Vecchio to the north side of the Arno River.

Merisi left the grounds of the palace and headed north. He took a boat across the river whose only other occupants were a young man and woman half-drunk with love and exhausted by passion.

Merisi was tired. Slowing his pace, he made his way back towards his unobtrusive, three-star accommodation in the Rapallo Hotel and entered its brightly lit foyer. He took a lift to his room and briefly leaned on the metal railing of his room's Juliet balcony, watching the night-time traffic trace the curve of the Giardino della Fortezza.

Having downed a glass of brandy and smoked a small cigar in his modest-sized room, Merisi undressed, arranging his clothes in a neat line—military fashion—on the spare twin bed. He took out a square device some four inches corner to corner from his inside jacket pocket. Rotating the illuminated dial so that the device would ensure that he slept for precisely sixty minutes, he caught sight of the alarm-clock-radio on the bedside table—a primitive electric timepiece that few people of his time had seen except in archive material.

How the world has progressed, he thought. *But progressed to what? Surely the whole concept of progress implies motion towards something, doesn't it? So where has this "progress" taken us? Towards the world's destruction?*

Merisi wondered whether his own grandfather might have used such a device. He held it up to the light and marvelled at the sheer weight of the plastic. He dismissively tossed the device on the spare bed, but the iconic object reminded him of his responsibility to make a better future for the world that he had just left. As he placed his altogether more sophisticated device with its prominent UNA logo on the pillow beside him, his thoughts turned once again to Shui Feng and the important task ahead of him.

Falling into bed, he turned off the two lights above his bedstead and gathered the sheet over his weary limbs. As the breeze from the balcony caused the long curtains to tremble, Merisi fell into a deep sleep. He dreamed he was on a street outside a busy inn, pinned to the ground by a screaming man accusing him of being an adulterer. Helping him were two men who claimed to be his brothers. They held him down while the man who was screaming carved a large *V* into his face.

As blood streamed from the wound, the attacker screamed again. *"Vendetta!"*

Merisi woke, his bedsheet soaked in sweat.

"Madre di Dio!" he cried. "Is there to be no end to this nightmare?"

CHAPTER 8

A BOOKSHOP
IN SIENA

Merisi composed himself, his attention focused on the
work in hand. His device told him that he had slept
forty-five minutes, but there was no more time for
recovery. A little more than ten minutes later, he strode from
the hotel entrance into the balmy Florentine night.

Merisi smiled as he saw the Lamborghini Veneno still parked
in the Via Roma, a small street that issued northwards from
the main piazza. By the standards of the day, the Veneno was
protected with state-of-the-art anti-theft devices, which was
probably why its owner had so brazenly parked the vehicle in full
view. The vehicle had no defence against twenty-second-century
technology, and Merisi soon had the engine purring quietly as
he picked his way through the pedestrian street of Florence's
historic central area.

Once clear of the city centre and out on the open road, man
and car sped almost silently south to Siena.

• •

Using his navigation device, Merisi drove to within fifty yards
of the facade of Siena's impressive medieval cathedral. There, he

discretely parked the Veneno in a side street and approached the cathedral on foot, moving stealthily in the shadows.

At three in the morning, the glare of the moon gave Siena's white cathedral a ghostly glow. The lower facade was built in the Tuscan Romanesque style and boasted three portals surmounted by lunettes and surrounded by intricate carvings of acanthus scrolls and figures from the Bible. Its design was simple and geometrical. The upper facade featured a circular rose window in the centre and was built much later in the more elaborate French Gothic style. At its top, a mosaic on the highest gable was illuminated by the moon. Designed by Luigi Mussini, it celebrated the heavenly coronation of the Virgin Mary, to whom the cathedral was dedicated.

Just to the right, the famed bell tower stood proud and tall, the black and white horizontal marble stripes a homage to the horses of Siena's founders, Senius and Aschius. To the left, a few steps from the bronze central portal known as the Porta della Riconoscenza, stood a column with a statue of the Contrade Lupa, the she-wolf who suckled Rome's founders, Romulus and Remus. Legend had it that Senius and Aschius, sons of Remus, stole this statue from the Temple of Apollo in Rome and brought it to Siena.

Crouching in a doorway beyond the reach of the moon's light on the other side of the Piazza del Duomo, Merisi watched in silence. The white suit that had fluoresced in the sunlight of Florence had transformed into a jumpsuit as black as his coarse beard. Merisi observed how the utterly black shadow cast by the column bearing the Contrade Lupa contrasted with the pale grey of the piazza on which it fell. On such a bright night, it would be easy to observe his target.

Merisi did not wait long. Just beyond the column, at ground level on the north side, a small stone glimmered with a phosphorescent light. This was not caused by the moon, nor by Bernini's gilded lantern atop the hexagonal dome. This was the incandescence of another world, a light that was very familiar to the agent watching from the shaded doorway. Letters that could easily have been missed by day or night gleamed on the stone, revealing a perfect square:

S	A	T	O	R
A	R	E	P	O
T	E	N	E	T
O	P	E	R	A
R	O	T	A	S

Suddenly, there appeared a small but athletic figure kneeling in front of the square symbol. Merisi instantly recognised the grim, determined face illuminated by the watery blue light. He rose from his haunches to better observe the scene.

Shui Feng looked up towards the moon as if preparing for some primal howl. The watcher in the doorway took half a pace back. Feng looked from side to side before rising and turning in one urgent movement. Soon, the lean assassin was marching with a brisk purposefulness, seemingly unconcerned that anyone might be watching. As Shui Feng slipped beneath the shadow of the column, Merisi briefly scanned the piazza to verify that Feng had indeed come alone through the portal. Merisi crept out into the pale light, hugging the buildings along the square. When he was satisfied that he was out of Feng's eyeline, he changed direction and followed the new arrival, who was now some fifty yards in front of him.

Suddenly, as if he sensed his pursuer, Feng was running, faster than it seemed a man could run, away from the western facade of the cathedral. Merisi followed at a cautious distance, remembering the stern warning not to engage.

Merisi tracked Feng as he moved swiftly down the Via del Castoro and several other streets and alleyways, until he reached a shop selling antique books. Merisi halted and hid behind the corner of a building at the end of street. He watched Feng take out a key from his tunic and unlock the front door. Feng slid like a phantom into its murky interior.

As the door of the bookshop closed, Merisi took out his silver lighter. "Target arrived. I have followed him to the centre of the old city, where he has entered a small bookshop—Acquapietre Libri," he whispered.

"Acquapietre Libri?" queried a woman's voice. "That is not a location that is known to us. Try to find out what he's doing in there, but proceed with extreme caution."

"Understood."

"Does it appear that he is alone?"

"Yes, he's definitely alone. I'm moving forward to look."

Merisi crept towards the entrance of the bookshop. Peering through the curved bay window into the darkness, he could just make out bookcases that rose to the ceiling with books crammed into their sagging shelves. In the faint beam of a dim security light, motes of dust fell slowly, disturbed by the breeze that followed Feng's brisk entrance.

There was no sign of Feng, so Merisi tried the front door. He smiled. The ultra-confident Feng had not locked the door behind him, being unburdened by fear and self-doubt. *That might bring about your downfall one day, you arrogant little shit!* thought Merisi as he quietly stepped onto the plush carpet of the shop.

He cast his eyes around the darkened space, made narrow by the deep wooden shelves on either side. The property extended some twenty-five yards from where he stood, and there a doorway led to another room.

Merisi cautiously moved towards the small room, which was a storeroom filled with yet more books. Feng was inside with his back to the door. Merisi watched him lift his right hand to his left ear. Feng depressed the centre of an inner ear monitor hidden beneath his jet-black hair. A tiny metal arm emerged from the body of the IEM. It extended from the side of his head and around towards his left eye. An oval eyepiece unfolded like a flag. It was black on the outside, but from Feng's perspective it swarmed with polychromatic digits and letters, casting a sickly green glow across the room.

Having digested the information transmitted from his eyepiece, Feng removed the equipment, folded it neatly and stashed it in a pocket. He then leaned firmly against the bookcase in front of him, which opened with a creak to reveal what appeared to be a garage. The walls were lined with tools, bicycle tyres and ladders, and cardboard boxes bursting with old books yet to be unpacked. Cooler, fresher air wafted in, providing relief from the unmistakeable musty smell of a thousand old books.

Merisi craned his neck to get a better view. He saw Feng remove a thick, round, silver object from a pocket in his black, soft-textile vest. It was the shape and size of a napkin ring. When he placed it on the stone floor, a cylinder of blue light rose, illuminating the entire space.

Feng moved purposefully towards a large holdall on a shelf stacked with bags and boxes. He withdrew a small Samurai sword with a black handle and black sheath. He then took out a wad of bank notes, a passport and some credit cards and placed each within the invisible pockets of his vest, taking care to reattach the fasteners. Finally, he strode to the far corner and removed a dustsheet from an object that was about three feet high, revealing a sleek and beautifully lined black Ducati 916 motorcycle.

Silence suddenly exploded with noise as a motorcycle engine revved—but it was not Feng's Ducati. The sound came from the front of the shop.

Merisi retreated behind a leather armchair just before Feng turned towards the source of the sound. Feng quickly extinguished the bright light from his device, crept out of the room and stood silently, his black leather boots a few feet from where Merisi was crouching.

The bike had stopped just outside the door of the bookshop. Suddenly, the engine cut off. Merisi heard footsteps and then the rasp of a key being inserted into a Yale lock, followed by surprised and animated voices, in Italian, as the unlocked door swung open. A man and woman entered; Merisi deduced that they must be the owners of the establishment. He also guessed that from the tone of the conversation they were a husband and wife, each blaming the other for forgetting to lock the door.

The fluorescent strip lights of the shop flickered and then

burst into blinding white light. The couple was in their thirties and dressed in matching beige-and-orange motorcycle leathers, each carrying a red, full-face helmet. They stopped in astonishment upon seeing the bold intruder standing motionless in the middle of their shop. After an open-mouthed gasp, the man raised his free arm in protest and advanced towards Feng, demanding in Italian to know what he was doing in his shop.

"STOP!" commanded Feng. "I am from the Health and Safety Executive, and I am here to tell you that you have neither— because I am going to kill you."

In a split second, the GIATCOM agent hit the man with a swift blow just below his left ear, fatally breaking his neck. The man's wife drew in a huge breath, and was about to scream, but was felled by a knife that bisected the frontal lobe of her brain before she could exhale.

Feng sauntered across the bookshop floor to retrieve the knife he had thrown, and briefly examined the slumped body of the woman's husband to make sure that he was dead. Then, he cleaned the bloodied knife on the carpet and returned to the back room to finish preparing the black Ducati.

Merisi, who had watched the murders with a mixture of professional admiration for Feng's efficiency, disgust at his cold ruthlessness, and horror at the potential repercussions for the future, decided that he had lingered for long enough, and that it was time for him to return to his primary duty in Florence. Seizing his opportunity, he leapt from behind the armchair and ran to the door of the storeroom. As he slammed the door shut, Merisi saw his adversary look up, alerted by the sound of footsteps, but Feng was too late. Merisi locked the solid oak door with the key that was still in the lock. He knew the locked door would not hold Feng at bay for long and probably wasn't the only exit, so he frantically slung a leg over the green-and-white Kawasaki Z750 parked just outside the door and sped off. Once safely away, he pulled over, drew the silver lighter halfway from his breast pocket and spoke into it.

"Returning to Florence. Feng has seen me and will no doubt be close behind."

• •

Merisi reclined into one of several cold metal chairs scattered on the terrace of the Caffè Gilli. It was approaching six in the morning. Although the rising summer sun was already illuminating the pale facade of the Hotel Savoy with a warm, golden glow, the centre of Florence had barely woken. The carousel in the Piazza della Repubblica was silent and still, and the last of the street cleaners had long since returned home after completing the night shift.

A grim-faced, bearded man, Merisi looked out of place on the terrace of the closed cafe, in that he conspicuously lacked any sign of relaxation. He didn't smoke. He didn't sip from a coffee cup. He did not chat idly to friends. Instead, he gazed ahead at the front entrance of the Hotel Savoy and surveyed the eastern half of the piazza, alert for any sign of movement. Remaining hidden in the shadows was no longer Merisi's priority. He was anxious now. Feng had arrived, and Merisi knew that it would not be long before he encountered his old foe once again.

CHAPTER 9

BREAKFAST IN FLORENCE

Ben Richards sat alone at breakfast by a window looking out onto the piazza. On his table was his usual healthy combination of granola, a yoghurt and a grapefruit juice. He looked relaxed, wearing an open-necked, navy-and-grey baroque shirt and a pair of casual cotton trousers. But his mind was preoccupied with his work and with the presentations that he would soon be giving.

He opened the folder—his constant companion, it seemed— and took out a typed document with the words *Lecture at the Energy Institute in Milan, April 5, Dr. Ben Richards, UCL* at the top. He flicked through the pages and removed a silver Montblanc biro from the breast pocket of his shirt and began making corrections and notes in the margins.

From time to time his eyes diverted to the street, drifting left from the shop front of the delicatessen opposite him to the main piazza, where the outdoor terraces of the hotels and cafes were populating with customers emerging for breakfast. He was about to turn back to his notes when he heard an animated voice behind him.

"This is indeed fortuitous!"

Richards turned to face a bald man with a pink face and a brow that betrayed a few beads of perspiration.

"I've been awake all night," said Tony Clarke, the football team manager.

"Oh, I'm sorry to hear that."

"No, no, no. It's good. It's really good. I'm excited, very excited."

Richards smiled. "Sounds like you need an espresso."

"No, what I really need is a few more moments of your precious time, Dr. Richards. I can't get your concept out of my head. But I need to ask just one or two more questions if I'm to sell this venture to my board."

Clarke didn't wait to be beckoned to the table. He drew out the only other chair and parked his substantial posterior on the cushion.

"Caffe latte," he barked at a passing waitress. "And bring me a plate of doughnuts."

Without even checking to see if she had heard him, Clarke thrust his head forward and blurted loudly, "Can't wait to get back home and have a full English breakfast!"

"When are you returning?"

"I'm flying out late morning."

"When's the board meeting?"

"Thursday, and I've already put your project on the agenda— main item."

"That is very good to hear," Richards said as he took another small spoonful of yoghurt.

"I see you're on the healthy stuff," Clarke observed.

"I like to start the day well," Richards replied.

The waitress arrived with a square plate, which she lowered in front of Clarke.

"For you, sir, I have the ciambella with custard, fritole with raisins, and bombolone with strawberry jam. Enjoy!"

Clarke tucked a large white serviette into the neck of his shirt and attacked the first doughnut.

"I like to have my five a day," said Clarke, puffing a small snowstorm of confectioner's sugar off the top of the bombolone. "Let me ask you again," he continued with not a hint of self-consciousness about speaking with his mouth full, "why, in particular, a football stadium roof should be the optimum location for your wind turbines."

"It's a good question," Richards replied. "Have you ever heard of the Coanda Effect?"

"What's that?"

"It's to do with fluid dynamics and the way in which a stream of air or water behaves as it flows over or across an object. Think for a moment about aeroplane wings. They are always curved at their front edge. Have you ever wondered why the wind follows these curvatures, flowing behind the wing to create aerodynamic lift?"

"Not really, no."

"The reason why your plane will take off this morning is because the wind will stick to the surface of a curved wing, flow behind the wing and be directed down to the ground, thereby creating the lift that pushes the plane up into the air. That, my friend, is the Coanda Effect, and it's the reason why you will not plummet to the earth and create your own strawberry jam on the tarmac."

"That's a cheerful thought," Clarke said, wiping jam from his purpling lips.

"The Coanda Effect is the tendency of a moving fluid, liquid or gas to hug a surface and flow along it."

"So, this applies to water as well as wind?"

"Yes. When you get home you can see for yourself. Grab a spoon from a kitchen drawer and hold it by the handle next to a running tap in the sink. Push the bowl end of the spoon gently towards the running water so that the back of the curved bowl has water running across it. Watch how the water's flow attaches to the curved surface of the spoon and follows it."

"That's all very interesting, but how does all this apply to football stadium rooves?" Clarke asked.

"If your board agrees to install my turbines, then the roof will be specially designed to my secret specs with curves like the wings of an airplane."

"Secret specs?"

"Yes. You need to design your roof very precisely," Richards said. "Then it'll function like an airplane wing and you'll be able to harness the best of the wind all of the time."

"What's the difference between those giant propellers in green fields and what you're talking about?"

"The problem with field or ocean turbines is that they frequently cut out. There are no surfaces over which the wind can pass. Too much wind, or sudden changes in wind, can cause the turbine blades to cut out and even sheer right off. Stadium roof turbines allow for a much more controlled laminar flow of wind because they maximise the full potential of the Coanda Effect."

"I think I'm beginning to see," said Clarke.

"If you get your roof shape right, then you will actually create a Coanda Effect, thereby ensuring a constant undisturbed wind flow, generating huge amounts of renewable energy for your own needs and for your community."

"So, how do we need to design our new roof?"

"You need to make sure that you curve it in an upward crest at the outer edges, thereby channelling the wind flow inward across the diameter of the roof, increasing its speed way beyond what is possible in a free flow of wind."

"That's clever," Clarke said, devouring the tail end of his second doughnut.

"Actually, it's really quite simple. Just remember the spoon and the running tap. Wind, like water, will be attracted to a convex curved surface and cling to it. That's what will happen on your stadium roof."

"So, what will our roof have to look like?"

"The ideal shape is an incline towards the centre, creating a slight dome effect with a hole in the middle, if you can picture it."

"I think so. But will wind turbines fitted to a stadium roof create more power than one large ground-mounted turbine installed close by?"

"Indeed they will. The key thing is that my turbines will manipulate the wind not only to channel it in the right direction but to increase its speed. You can't do that with a ground or sea-mounted turbine."

"And you have proof of this?"

"My turbines have yet to be properly tested, but I am absolutely convinced that this works, and that this is not only what you need, but also what your community and indeed the planet needs."

"You seem very sure."

"It's a win-win situation, Tony."

"I have another question," Clarke said. "Why don't we just install solar PVs on our new roof?"

"Simple," Richards replied. "The energy efficiency from solar panel can be anything between 12 to 18 percent. Guess how much it is from my wind turbines?"

"I have no idea."

"It's nearer 40 percent. Double the efficiency from wind power means double the energy distributed and sold to your community, and you gain more feed in tariff as a result."

"Couldn't we have both solar PVs and wind turbines?"

"There's no reason why you can't maximise the full potential of your roof space and have a number of solar PVs as well as a large wind-turbine array, provided your roof is designed correctly."

"I see," said Clarke. "And how much will it cost us to install a wind-turbine array?"

"The figures are in the brochure I gave you last night. It's about seventy grand for an 18-kilowatt turbine system consisting of three 6-kilowatt units. Also, remember what I wrote there; this sort of system is much cheaper in the long run than free-standing wind turbines, the giant propellers you mentioned."

"And what else would we need?"

"The main thing you'd need to do is upgrade your existing electricity distribution board within your transformer substation at the stadium."

"That sounds a bit technical."

"Put as simply as I can, after the direct current produced by a generator converts mechanical energy from wind turbines to electricity, the direct current is inverted to an alternating current. The upgraded transformer then reduces the high voltage to low voltage and distributes electricity via a board to different appliances and end-users."

"I think I see."

As Clarke wiped his sweaty brow with a white napkin, a noisy refuse lorry pulled up just outside the hotel window.

Richards took a final sip of his grapefruit juice. He was about to pick up his lecture notes when he felt a hand on his shoulder. Even before he saw her, he knew from the scent it was Grazia Rossini. She leaned and whispered in his ear.

"We have to go—now!"

Richards stood suddenly, knocking the table with his knee and throwing his empty glass into the air.

Rossini dove like a gymnast to successfully catch the glass an inch from the floor, sprawled out flat on her back in the middle of the restaurant floor. Other patrons gawked in silence.

"What's a matter, Doctor? Haven't you seen a girl do yoga before?" She sprang back to her feet with a kip-up. "It's good I'm wearing my trouser suit today, or my skirt would have been ripped." She smiled.

Clarke dropped his fork and mouth while Richards shook his head.

"That's quite a little party trick you've got there, Grazia," Richards said. "You'll have to excuse us, Tony, but Ms. Rossini and I have a long journey ahead."

"Quite understandable," Clarke said. "I have your contact details."

"Good luck with the board meeting," Richards said, shaking Clarke's hand. "And good luck with the new stadium and your first season in the Premier League."

"Thanks! People are telling me that we're going to need a miracle to stay up; maybe I have just found that miracle! If I am unable to generate sufficient ticket sales, I could create revenue from selling energy, to be able to buy better players."

With a cheerful smile and a wave of his left hand, he turned and left.

Rossini tugged Richards by the elbow and placed her hand in his arm, drawing him away from the table and the window of the restaurant just as the refuse lorry pulled away. Rather surprised by the young journalist's forwardness, Richards allowed himself to be frog-marched into the foyer.

"Are your bags packed?" she asked.

"Yes, I've left them in the hotel office, at reception."

Rossini led him to the reception desk. "Dr. Richards is checking out," she said. A small, uniformed middle-aged woman typed his details into the hotel computer.

"Thanks for rescuing me from Homer Simpson and his doughnuts," Richards smiled, wondering why the urgency for him to check out.

Rossini pulled him close. "We need to leave," she whispered. "When I was getting dressed this morning, I noticed a man sitting on the terrace in the cafe across the street. I don't trust him. Something was not quite right about him. Behave normally."

"Well, did you recognise him or something?"

"No, his face was hidden from view."

"But I daresay that there will be many people in the cafes at this time in the morning. You sure he wasn't just having his breakfast?" Richards asked.

"The cafe across the street does not open until seven thirty, and he was just sitting there facing the hotel entrance. When you're a journalist, you notice these things. And in Italy you must be wary of men who sit in cafes or stand on street corners just watching and observing things."

Richards turned to the desk clerk and handed over his key and his credit card.

As soon as Richards had picked up his suitcase and shoulder bag, Rossini escorted him past the concierge and out the rear door of the hotel. Within seconds, they were hurrying down the street and into an alleyway.

"Here," she said, pointing to an Audi roadster with a jet-black bonnet. "Put your bags on the rear seat, and get in."

Richards opened the passenger door and climbed into the black leather seat. Rossini slipped into the driver's seat and started the engine. The screen of the virtual cockpit situated behind the three-spoke steering wheel flared to life. She flicked a switch and the screen switched to "infotainment" mode.

"Milan," she said.

The MMI navigation system kicked in. "315 kilometres," a robotic voice said. "Driving time: three hours, twenty minutes."

Rossini thrust the black, perforated gear lever into drive and pressed her foot on the aluminium accelerator. The quattro engine growled and the car sprang up the alley towards the street running behind the hotel. As Grazia steered onto the crowded road, she manoeuvred between the early shoppers and tourists now beginning their day.

"This may take a few minutes," she said. "People are not allowed to drive in the old city unless they have permission from the police."

"Do *we*?" Richards enquired.

"Let's just say I have friends."

"If someone is after me, then shouldn't we talk to your friends, especially if they're police?"

"They won't act on intuitions. They'll only respond if there's hard evidence."

"Isn't the attempt on my life yesterday and the dart evidence?"

"Maybe, but it doesn't tell us who shot it."

"What makes you think that this man might be after *me*?"

"Because when you went down to breakfast, I saw him move seats so that he could see you better."

Richards fell silent as he contemplated everything that Rossini had said. She too was deep in thought and said nothing as she negotiated the cramped streets of the old city centre. Eventually, to the relief of both, the quattro turned onto the autostrada. Rossini eased the engine into fifth gear, and they sped north towards Milan.

CHAPTER 10

CITY OF A MILLION WINDOWS

CHONGQING, CHINA

The sun began its descent beyond the city of a million windows. Standing tall in the middle of a landscape of paved stone, hundreds of glass buildings rose like stalagmites towards the scudding clouds, their sides gleaming in the orange of the setting sun.

A digital screen in the heart of the city, one hundred stories high, displayed a mauve jet-car that not only darted between cloud-high buildings but also dived beneath a turquoise sea, propelling itself like a torpedo around underwater atolls and coral gardens.

"You know you want it," a Thai girl with a tight black skirt said with a wink.

Another wink and the millions of pixels morphed into a picture of a towering edifice designed like an ancient ziggurat, its steps ascending towards a pyramid-shaped summit. At the tip was a giant logo of a hammer with lightning bolts shooting from both ends of its head. Underneath it, in red letters, the word *GIATCOM* glistened.

A man dressed in a pearly suit appeared on the screen. He stood behind a long crystal desk underneath a warm, pulsating light, his teeth as milky as his slacks.

"GIATCOM," he declared. "Power for the people."

As the smiling man faded from view, images emerged of nuclear power plants, in bleak Nordic wastelands one moment, burning Saharan deserts the next.

"GIATCOM," the man's voice boomed again. "Safe, clean, long-lasting energy."

A heartbeat later the screen had disappeared.

A long yellow vehicle slowed amidst a thousand airborne cars. It hovered alongside a platform on top of a building that rose like a chrome rocket 1,000 metres from the ground. Two doors slid open with a quiet hiss at the front of the black-lined coach, and fifty children, all dressed in white uniforms, poured onto the staging area to be ushered up a flight of steps onto a terrace above.

As the sun slid slowly down in the distance, the children put on glasses and listened to a teacher as their lenses streamed data to their retinas.

"The pyramid you see on your right is the global headquarters of GIATCOM Industries," she read. "It is the highest building in the world."

The children cooed.

"GIATCOM is now the only provider of nuclear power and supplies fuel for the entire planet. It has reactors in every sector of our world."

The teacher paused and pointed to the top of the ziggurat.

"At the summit you can see the logo for GIATCOM Industries. It shows the Mjolnir, the hammer of the ancient Nordic god called Thor. *Mjolnir* means 'that which pulverises to dust.'"

The children gasped.

"GIATCOM has pioneered a dynamic waste-management system that is no longer dependent on deep borehole disposal. It has also constructed safety-enhanced reactors. GIATCOM offers us fuel for the future.

"GIATCOM has replaced all other power-generating industries and has saved the planet from the effects of global warming through its use of carbon-free technology. Our one-world leaders decided that GIATCOM will be the exclusive source of nuclear power and have shut down all other suppliers, thereby removing the risk of maverick groups developing weapons-usable plutonium."

The children clapped.

"Thanks to the funding and oversight of our one-world leaders, nuclear power is now safe and cost-effective."

The children cheered. When they grew quiet, the teacher spoke again.

"Nuclear power is here to stay."

As she concluded, a white jump-jet limo escorted by four police officers on hover bikes pulled up at the ramp vacated by the yellow coach.

Two of the officers dismounted and stood guard as the driver's door, festooned with the GIATCOM logo, gradually opened. A chauffeur in a silver cap, silver shoes and silver suit disembarked. The golden GIATCOM hammer gleamed on his breast pocket as he waited.

"Cheer!" the teacher said through their earpieces.

The children obeyed.

As their volume matched their anticipation, a tall and well-built American man deplaned and stood at ease on the ramp. He was followed by a woman with long tanned legs and swept-back strawberry-blonde hair. She wore an ivory knee-length dress that hugged her contours like an extra layer of skin. She hooked herself to the man's arm and smiled at the applauding schoolchildren. They were yelling now.

But there was something wrong.

The man frowned.

His posture stiffened as he noticed that the children were staring behind and beyond him towards the dying sun. And they were screaming.

As he turned, the man's eyes widened. There in the distance a bright white flash transfigured the landscape. The man hurriedly put on thick, dark glasses before bellowing an order and diving back into the limo. The woman calmly followed as the limo's doors locked shut and shields slid down the windows like membranes over a white shark's eyes.

The limo-jet and its police escort lifted off vertically, speeding in the opposite direction of the blast. A few seconds later a gargantuan cloud billowed towards the heavens, its unbroken stem reaching up with unstoppable momentum from the ground. The prodigious cloud continued to ascend like a grey and ghastly floret. Then the sound of a detonating bomb, travelling slower than the speed of light, assaulted the city.

At first there was a deafening boom. Then, a primal growl moved from the horizon towards the ziggurat. It intensified, shaking the foundations, breaking every window throughout the doomed metropolis.

A violent blast of wind like fiery breath from the nostrils of a dragon blew the children and their teacher from their feet. They struggled for breath as they wiped their flash-blinded eyes.

And then it came.

As the growl became an unbearable roar, a tsunami shockwave full of white-hot fire swept through the city, incinerating every one of the children in a nanosecond, vaporising their groping forms.

••

"Are you alright, Ben?" enquired a woman's voice in a pleasing Italian accent.

Richards' entire body jolted as if he too had been hit by the force of the bomb. Then, his eyes opened, and he was wide awake. His hands trembled as he looked through the windscreen of the Audi Roadster, staring at the tarmac disappearing beneath the black bonnet. All around were the fertile fields and hills of the Tuscan countryside.

Grazia Rossini was holding his wrist.

"Are you okay?"

"Yes, I'm okay."

"Really?"

"I was just having a bad dream."

"What did you see just now?"

"Nothing . . . really," he stammered.

"It didn't sound like nothing. You were groaning before I woke you up."

"I was?"

"Tell me."

"It was just a dream."

"Dreams are doors, Ben, doors to our heart, and gateways to other worlds."

"I'm an engineer, not a mystic."

"Even engineers dream. Do you often have vivid dreams like that?"

"Sometimes," he replied. "It happens quite a lot, actually, and not just when I'm asleep."

"Oh? You mean you hallucinate?"

"I'm not sure. I wouldn't call it hallucinating, exactly, but I definitely see things. Things that cannot be real. It could be a very mundane object, but to me it appears to be something else. I've been like that since I was a kid."

"Is this something that has ever been diagnosed? It sounds like it might be a psychosis of some kind."

Richards snorted. "Of course not. It's nothing. It's just a childhood thing that has never left me. I'm probably just a daydreamer, that's all."

"It sounds like you're an only child," said Rossini with a knowing smile.

Richards glanced at the young Italian, feeling a little uncomfortable with her intrusiveness yet quietly impressed with her incisive journalistic mind. In fact, her demeanour placed him at ease. She was not judging him. She seemed to just have a very lively curiosity. It was not difficult for Richards to feel that she had a genuine interest in him.

"Well, are you?" she persisted.

"An only child?"

"Yes."

Richards paused. "Yes," he said, with his eyes fixed on the road ahead.

"I thought so," she said with a triumphant smile. "That means that you will have spent a long time on your own, learning how to keep your mind occupied. I am an only child myself. I bet you're the type of person who never gets bored. I expect there's always something happening in that brain of yours."

Again, Richards was impressed. He didn't feel the necessity to tell Rossini that she was right, but her diagnosis was spot on.

"I spent a lot of time on my own when I was young," he said. "My father died before I really knew him, and then I lost my mother in a tragic accident when I was eight."

"Oh, I am so sorry, Ben," she said. "I didn't mean to—"

"It was a long time ago."

The pair fell silent as Richards stirred in his seat and put on his Ray-Bans to shield his tired eyes from the bright and cloudless sky.

"But tell me about your dream," insisted Rossini after a while. "Come on, Ben. Tell me what you saw."

Richards sighed.

"I saw death. I saw an entire city destroyed, children vaporised, buildings shredded like meat. It felt like the end of the world."

"Do you mean this world?"

"It didn't look like our world. It felt like another dimension altogether, like a city in a parallel universe. Everything was more advanced."

"How do you mean?"

"Cars were airborne, and buildings were better designed, better fitted, and they were all taller than the one in Dubai, much taller."

"You mean the Burj Khalifa?" she asked.

"And the explosion."

"Explosion?"

"It completely drowned out the sun, obliterated everything, even the great pyramid."

"Pyramid?"

"A huge pyramid right in the centre of the city; it was the tallest of all the buildings."

"Describe it to me."

"It seemed to be the headquarters for a nuclear power company called GIATCOM. Have you heard of it?" Richards asked.

"It's not on my list of the forty-plus power plants I've investigated. That said, the current nuclear renaissance is spawning new units all the time, and somewhere among these fourth-generation projects there may be a GIATCOM waiting in the wings."

"You're talking as if my dream corresponds to reality," Richards said.

"Maybe it does, maybe it doesn't. But at the very least it shows that your involvement in non-thermal power is more than simply scientific."

"What do you mean?"

"I mean your motives for advocating wind technology are partly emotional."

Richards removed his sunglasses and wiped their lenses with a clean handkerchief.

"You sound like a shrink."

"I'm not objecting," Rossini said. "I think there are many very strong reasons for feeling scared about the future."

"It's a dangerous world our children are growing up in," Richards said.

"Do you have any children?"

"No, I've never married."

"Are you scared of committing to someone?"

"No, that's not it."

"Then what is it?"

Richards squirmed. "This is a bit too intimate for me," he said. "I'm a scientist."

"Life is more than a set of equations," Rossini said.

Richards sighed. "You're not going to let me avoid your question, are you?"

Rossini laughed and shook her head. "No, I'm not."

"Well then, I confess. I am a little afraid."

"Afraid of what?"

"Not commitment," Richards said.

"Then what?"

"I'm afraid of not being believed."

Grazia paused. "Where does that come from?"

Richards reached for the infotainment screen and located a radio station playing 1970s rock. It was Joy Division playing "Shadow Play," a favourite from his youth. "I just love this one!"

Rossini frowned in mock annoyance when Richards turned up the volume. She slowed the car enough for the roof to be lowered as he sang along to the lyrics.

> To the centre of the city, where all the roads
> meet, waiting for you;
> To the depths of the ocean, where all hopes
> sank, searching for you;
> I was moving through the silence without
> motion, waiting for you;
> In a room with a window, in the corner, I found
> truth.
>
> In the shadow play, acting out your own death,
> knowing no more;
> As the assassins all grouped into four lines,
> dancing on the floor;
> And with cold steel, odour on their bodies,
> made a move to connect;
> But I could only stare in disbelief, as the clouds
> all left.
>
> I did everything, everything I wanted to;
> I let them use you for their own ends;
> To the centre of the city in the night, waiting for
> you;
> To the centre of the city in the night, waiting
> for you.

"Assassins?" queried Rossini as she glanced at her rearview mirror. "I do hope that's not a prophetic lyric."

"What do you mean?"

"We're being followed," she said, pressing the accelerator. "Green Kawasaki, one hundred metres behind us. It's been following us for half an hour."

"How do you know?"

"It's observed exactly the same speed as us."

"Is it the man from outside the hotel?"

"It's difficult to say with his helmet on, but I'm not taking any chances."

"You can't outrun a motorcycle," Richards said.

"Just watch me."

CHAPTER 11

ARRIVAL IN MILAN

Only when the sun-soaked motorway reached the outskirts of Milan did Grazia speak again.

"I think we have lost him, but we should take a detour."

"What kind of detour?"

"We should make as if we're heading into the city from the south, but then head north and enter Milan from the west side."

"Why?"

"If anyone's waiting along the predictable route, they will be disappointed."

"Clever," Richards said.

"And besides, I'm sure you'd welcome a quick look at the San Siro."

"Bravo!" Richards exclaimed. "You're killing two birds with one stone."

"I just thought you might like to see the stadium. And one more thing, Ben; I think it would be wise if I cancelled your hotel room and we stayed somewhere safer."

"Have you somewhere in mind?"

"My cousin has an apartment near the Piazza del Duomo, and I have a key. She's away and I have use of the place when she's out of town."

"That's all good, but whoever's following us is bound to know where and when I'm speaking tomorrow."

"I'm sure they do," Rossini said. "But I see no reason to make it any easier for them in the meantime."

Richards smiled as they left the aptly named Motorway of the Sun and headed towards suburbs packed with 1950s and '60s industrial buildings boasting billboards and neon signs.

Rossini drove north until she swerved without warning down an inconspicuous road heading west along grey-paved streets with embedded tramlines, bordered by row upon row of trees in full leaf. They stopped at a pedestrian crossing to wait for a dreamy cyclist to meander over the road while a small white dog yapped and pulled at its owner's lead, reaching towards the relief of a tree.

On they went through traffic lights and trees, avoiding horse-drawn carriages and plodding buses. Fifteen minutes later Rossini skirted a convoy of mopeds, and there, looming in front of them, was the towering San Siro Stadium.

"It's an interesting design, isn't it?" Grazia remarked as she applied the brakes. "We really have Italia '90 to thank for it."

"How?"

"When Italy was made the hosts for the 1990 World Cup, it was obvious the San Siro wasn't big enough for World Cup matches, so three Italian architects were enlisted to build a third tier of seating."

Richards studied the cylinders running up the four corners and sides of the building.

"I see how they did it," he remarked. "They used those cylindrical towers."

"Precisely; there are eleven of them, all made of reinforced concrete."

"And I presume they not only support the new third level but also the roof," Richards added.

"That's right. The four angular towers are over fifty metres high and, unlike the other seven, they ascend beyond the third level to act as supports for the roof's main beams, those huge red metallic girders you can see along the perimeter of the stadium and intersecting at the four corners. They are nearly ten metres high."

Richards sighed. "Unfortunately, there's no curvature built into that design."

"Don't be too downcast. There are proposals for completing the third tier. There's seating on the north, south and west sides but not the east. If that happens, they may have to redesign the roof."

Grazia removed her sunglasses as the car stopped behind a white bus. She turned to Richards and smiled.

"That's why I have taken the liberty to invite the vice presidents of both teams to your lecture tomorrow."

"You're joking!"

"I am not," Rossini laughed. "And furthermore, they've not only agreed. They've also invited us to the Derby della Madonnina."

"Is that what I think it is?"

"If you're thinking the match between Inter Milan and A.C. Milan, then yes."

Richards smiled. "You are truly remarkable," he said, reaching across the gear stick and stroking her bare arm.

Rossini raised her eyebrows, surprised at the professor's gesture of affection. She smiled, locking on his eyes before replacing her sunglasses and driving towards the city centre.

Four kilometres later they were passing delis and department stores, banks and boutiques.

"This is the financial and fashion centre of Italy," she said. "People say that Milan has less soul than Florence. But the cathedral is a lasting counterargument, wouldn't you say?"

Richards stared out at the Gothic duomo with its pearly facade and prodigious stained-glass windows. He marvelled at the statues and spires that rose from every available space, reaching like adoring hands towards the copper statue of the crowned Madonna, the protector of the city, adorning the summit.

"It certainly makes a statement," he said.

Rossini steered the car away from the cathedral piazza and followed a moped with two riders down a side street. She turned off the street and down a ramp into an underground car park. She parked the roadster in the shadow of a bright-white Evoque and opened the Audi's trunk.

"Follow me," she said, passing Richards his bag.

Grazia marched towards a door thirty metres away.

Richards glanced at the cars as he followed her—gleaming Mercedes, BMWs, Alfa Romeos, several Bugattis and even a navy-blue Aston Martin DB9. In fact, there was no sign of a Panda or a Punto anywhere. These were apartments for the affluent, urban pads for those on pilgrimage to La Rinascente, perhaps—the city's prestigious department store at the Piazza del Duomo where the nation's most sought-after designer clothes could be found.

Once through the door, they entered a lift and ascended to the top floor of the building.

"Here it is," she said as the door slid open.

Rossini strode across a marble hallway and then turned down a gold-carpeted corridor. She stopped outside apartment 32 and reached inside her black messenger bag for her keys.

A moment later the door was open, and they were inside.

"Make yourself at home. I'll phone the hotel and cancel. Was it the Hotel Square?"

"Yes," Richards replied. "It's called the Square Milano Duomo."

Rossini located the number on her smartphone and then dialled the apartment phone.

As Rossini spoke to a receptionist, Richards walked into the living room. There was a white marble fireplace to his left with a black TV mounted on the wall above it. Two red armchairs, more ornamental than functional, stood on either side of the hearth, facing away from the TV and towards a glass coffee table in the centre of the room. It was covered in fashion magazines. Beyond the table, to Richards' right, there was a long red sofa.

Rossini finished her call and pulled the lace curtains across two tall windows. He saw her eyes flicking to the couch and then back at him.

"You're in here," she said as she walked over to release the lever at the back of the couch and extend a bed out into the middle of the floor.

She opened a door in the corner of the room and beckoned Richards to see where she would be staying. The room beyond was spacious and clean, with a king-sized bed against the far wall. As in the living room, the walls were painted in soothing white and dove-grey palettes, and the floor was sleek wood.

"Now, Dr. Richards, we must respect each other's privacy and professionalism and focus on the task in hand and keeping you safe. We wouldn't want to lose focus, now, would we, Doctor?"

Richards nodded, now slightly embarrassed by his flirtation in the car.

Above the bedstead was a shelf with two candles, one at each end, and a small, state-of-the-art music centre in the middle, with an iPod dock. Above it, a painting hung on the wall. It depicted a futuristic cityscape in yellow, white, beige and gold, with airborne planes and zeppelins and speeding underground and over-ground trains.

"It's an original oil painting called *Architettura*," Grazia said.

"Who's the artist?"

"Tullio Crali. He was a self-taught painter and also a stunt pilot."

"I don't know of him."

"He was influenced by Filippo Marinetti, the founding father of futurism, one of Milan's most famous sons. Like many futurist artists, Crali was fascinated by flight, speed, energy and the like."

"It's quite eerie, even if it's bold and simple," Richards remarked.

"Crali painted it in the late 1930s, but he clearly imagined the future," she said.

"How did your cousin come by it?"

"Before he died here in Milan fifteen years ago, Crali gave this smaller version of the original oil painting to her as a gift."

"They were lovers?"

Rossini smiled. "Not every gift is an act of foreplay, Ben."

Richards chuckled. "It must be worth a bit," he said.

"My estimate is between fifty and one hundred thousand US dollars."

"I'd better be careful then."

"My cousin would appreciate it," Rossini laughed.

Richards lowered his valise onto the bed and unpacked his wash bag and a fresh shirt.

"Mind if I have a quick shower?"

"Go right ahead." Rossini smiled. "I'm just going out to the shop, to get a few things."

As she closed the door behind her, Richards stripped. He grabbed his wash bag and opened the door to the en suite. As soon as he entered a ceiling light automatically activated, illuminating the clean and minimalist decor inside. He climbed into the shower cubicle and turned the silver dial from medium to hot. As the showerhead released streams of water, he moved deeper into the glass booth, bowing beneath the warming jets.

A few minutes later he had lathered and cleansed his body and was about to turn the shower off when he noticed something through the steam-smeared glass.

There, in the doorway, was a figure standing perfectly still.

"Grazia, is that you?" Richards shouted.

There was no answer.

He turned the shower off and wiped his eyes. Still, the figure refused to move.

Richards opened the cubicle and peered round its edge. The door to the en suite was open and a full-length bathrobe was hanging on a hook.

"You idiot, Richards!" he cried. "Call yourself a man of science!"

He laughed as he wrapped the white robe around his moist body and made his way out of the bathroom. It was only as he turned and looked towards the door to the living room that he saw him.

There, at the threshold to the living room, was a black-haired man in a white suit. He stood with his arms folded, staring into Richards' eyes, a smile breaking out within the bounds of his immaculately trimmed facial hair.

Richards saw a scar on the man's face—two vivid grooves from his jawline to the shadow under his left eye, shaped like the letter *V*.

Grazia! Richards shuddered. "What have you done with her?" he exclaimed.

CHAPTER 12

MERISI'S REVELATION

The man in the white suit drew his jacket to one side, revealing a holstered pistol.

"Please sit down, Doctor," he said, beckoning to the sofa nearby.

"Where's Grazia?"

"She is shopping," the man answered.

"I don't believe you."

"Then look at this," the man said, withdrawing what looked like a small compact mirror from his belt. He ran his hand across it like a skilled magician, its screen facing Richards. There in the centre was Grazia shopping with a hand basket slung over her arm in a supermarket.

"You see, Doctor, she is perfectly safe. Now, please sit down."

"So, who are you, and where did you come from?" Richards moved into the living room towards the sofa and lowered himself onto its plush red cushion, keeping his eyes fixed on the intruder.

"Well, *when* I am from might be a more pertinent question," the man said, chuckling quietly as he paced to the window. He faced Richards. "My name is Merisi, and you, Doctor Richards, are a very important man—more important than you realise."

"What on earth do you mean?"

"I have little time to explain. Time, in fact, is of the essence here," Merisi replied.

"Then tell me what you want."

"Very well," said Merisi. "What I am about to share with you will stretch your credulity. But I am going to ask you to keep an open mind."

Richards sighed and nodded. "What choice do I have?"

Merisi smiled. "So, let me start by saying that, despite the grand march of science, there are many things in this universe that you do not yet understand. Not just in this universe, in fact, but in others parallel to and indeed in advance of this."

Richards raised both eyebrows.

"I see you are a sceptic," Merisi said.

"I prefer science fact to science fiction," Richards replied.

"OK. So, you are a 'scientist'?"

"Of course!"

"So, if I were to tell you something about myself that your entire being—your mind and soul—told you was impossible, then I take it that you wouldn't believe me."

Richards shrugged and said nothing.

"Still sceptical I see," continued Merisi. "What if I were to show you or do something that you considered to be impossible? Then you would have no choice but to believe it."

"Such as what?" asked Richards.

"Well, let's talk about that painting by Crali that you and the young lady were discussing just a few minutes ago."

"But how did you know that we were—"

"That is not important, Doctor," said Merisi with a dismissive wave. "The point is, what if I were to tell you that I could put you into that painting so that you could experience that future vision as a reality?"

"I would certainly retain a healthy scepticism," replied Richards, smugly.

"But if I then did so, and you were actually *there*, then you would have to acknowledge that it was possible," insisted Merisi.

"Well," replied Richards, "my first thought would be that you had probably created an illusion, or that you gave me a drug to make me hallucinate."

"Ah! That's a good point. So maybe that is not a very good example. As a matter of fact, I *could* give you a drug that would achieve that, but let's deal with one thing at a time."

Merisi surveyed the scene outside the window of the apartment once again before pacing towards the sofa.

"So, I will come to the point, Dr. Richards. What if I were to tell you that I have come from the future—the year 2112, to be precise—and that within a few hours, the three of us could be taking tea together in 2112 in a location far from here?"

"Well," Richards began, "I would naturally require some proof—"

"Proof! PROOF!" roared Merisi, throwing his head back and laughing with mocking disdain. "You mean to say that you would like this to be 'scientifically proven'? Let me tell you, Dr. Richards, that those two words form the most retarding expression in the history of the world. Of course, you are a slave to the conventions of normative science and determinism. You—or should I say *we*—should have listened more to the science fiction writers and less to the scientists!"

"But travelling through time—"

"Is impossible," interrupted Merisi. "Let me ask you a question, Doctor. Who would you say was the greatest human being to walk the earth over the past 2,000 years?"

"Okay," replied Richards, "Albert Einstein!"

"A good choice, Doctor," declared Merisi. "Einstein certainly came very close to the truth. Two of the truest statements he made were, 'Imagination is the highest form of research,' and 'Imagination is everything; it is the preview of life's coming attractions.' Unfortunately, he became much more famous and feted for his theories and his equations. Hawking, too, made a very important discovery about black holes."

"What was that?" asked Richards.

"That he, and the world, did not understand them, and that they were a phenomenon that science could not explain. Sometimes, seeing and stating the obvious—that we simply didn't know, in this case—is the first step to enlightenment, and that certainly turned out to be the case. I can give you another important quotation from your time," continued Merisi. "Robert A. Heinlein said, 'Everything is theoretically impossible, until it is done.'"

"*Heinlein*? I have not heard of him," said Richards.

"Of course not. That's because he was a science fiction writer—not a scientist. Heinlein also pointed out that it was possible to recount the history of science, in reverse, by listing all the things that people in authority said could not be done."

Richards took a moment to reflect.

"And you will have heard of Michelangelo Caravaggio, Dottore?"

"The painter? Yes, of course!"

"Well, let me tell you," continued Merisi. "Caravaggio was not just a great painter, but also a great man. A great thinker, and a man who had a better insight into life and the human condition than any man I have met."

"That you've *met*?"

"Yes, I *met* him. In fact, I was an acquaintance of his for three months. It was one of our earliest experiments in time travel. Our objective was to prove that it was possible to transport a humanoid back in time, and then bring him back after a predetermined period. Of course, I had to keep a very low profile, remaining as inconspicuous as possible, so I posed as his neighbour while I was there. He was a very difficult man to get to know. When the mood took him, he'd think nothing about waving a sword in your face and challenging you to a duel—a legacy of working with lead-based paint, I think. Eventually, we became friends, and I had many long and interesting conversations with him over a carafe of wine, or two."

Richards was struck by the similarity between Merisi and the famous self-portrait of Caravaggio.

"I can actually see a likeness," he said.

"Yes," replied Merisi. "I suppose I have rather modelled my appearance on the great man. And the name *Merisi* that I have taken for myself was Caravaggio's middle name, and the name that he liked to be called by close friends. That's a fact that you will not find in your history books."

"So, what can an inhabitant of the twenty-second century learn from a dead painter?" asked Richards.

"A great deal, my friend. Don't underestimate the power of ancient wisdom. Yes, the technology of humans made tremendous strides in the twenty-first and twenty-second centuries. We became the masters of time, and we had already conquered the process of our own reproduction, with human beings and other humanoid forms being produced to order. It would be more accurate to say *developed* than *born*."

"What do you mean by that?"

"Well, I was once a human being like yourself—more or less. By that I mean that a human being gave birth to me."

"You are talking about your *mother*!" exclaimed Richards, rather shocked that Merisi was able to speak in such dispassionate terms.

"Technically, yes," Merisi said, "but I did not have the same relationship with my birth mother that you had with yours."

Merisi saw that Richards was finding it hard to grasp the concept.

"Let's just say, Dottore, that my *father* was *the military*, and that my conception and everything that followed it was part of a carefully planned and targeted process. You might say that my journey towards being an *enhanced human* began when I was still in the birth mother's womb, and I became a trainee the moment that I drew my first breath of air."

"I get it. So, you were never destined to become a poet or an accountant, and there was never any chance of you running away to join a circus," quipped Richards.

"Quite so, Dottore. But I have always been a human being, and was brought up as one, training alongside other humans of my cohort. Although many of my physical and mental functions are enhanced by technologies that you will not be able to understand, I am a human being. I have a soul."

"But it does sound like a fairly dangerous use of technology to me," Richards said. "What if one of you enhanced humans decided to go rogue? I should imagine that you could do a great deal of damage."

"Quite so. But this rarely, if ever, happens because of our commitment to our values, which are based on contributing to the common good, and because we have always cherished the ever-diminishing part of us that is human. You will not be aware of this, Dottore, but it is in the very nature of artificial intelligence to fuel its own development, and to gradually replace the brain's original functions. The mechanisms that control physical strength and dexterity, which are controlled from within the spinal cord, behave in a very similar way. In fact, my development has included the installation and maintenance of important algorithms limiting the extent to which certain programmes can self-develop and mutate. Without those, I might lose my humanity altogether."

"It sounds terrifying!" said Richards.

"Quite! But you are perfectly safe in my presence, Dottore. However, I cannot say the same thing about the androids that might be sent here. They are far more dangerous."

"Wow! You have androids where you're from?" marvelled Richards.

"My world is crawling with them. Androids have been developed for all manner of things. You really can't imagine it, Dottore. But there is one that I am very wary of—Feng. He is a particularly nasty specimen."

"Feng?"

"Yes, Shui Feng. Well, that's a name that he has adopted. His true identity is a series of numbers. He is an android. More than that, he is designed to be an assassin. Not only has he been manufactured with superhuman strength, he is also equipped with a very high level of intelligence."

"Artificial intelligence, presumably?"

"Well, Dottore, when it comes down to it, there's not a great deal of difference between artificial intelligence and whatever it is humans are born with, especially when you get to a certain level of sophistication. After all, your brain—even *my* brain—is merely an organ for creating electrical impulses and distributing them throughout the body."

Richards raised an eyebrow, unable to challenge Merisi's statement.

"What these bastard machines *don't have* is any trace of humanity. We haven't yet managed to find a way of programming that into them. In fact, Feng probably has a sub-programme that is designed to destroy any shred of humanity in his circuits should one develop by mistake!"

"But he is merely a machine, right?"

"Well, technically, all humans are just *machines*, albeit biological ones and very advanced. But yes, Feng is a purely a product of the sciences of mankind. He has no true consciousness—save for the artificial consciousness that he has been provided with to enable him to carry out his functions. He is not *one of us*, Dottore. He has no concern for the fate of mankind, and no empathy for individuals. I have to admit that throughout the ongoing process of my enhancement, which has continued for many more years than I am prepared to admit to you, I have been installed with much of the same technology that enables Feng to perform at such a high level. But I have vowed to retain as much of my *humanity* as I can. I am determined that I will not end up like Feng. All of us on my enhancement programme felt the same way.

"Anyway, I first came across him when I went with half a dozen of my fellow trainees to investigate suspicious movements at a nuclear power plant. Feng was waiting for us. I was the lucky one—apparently. All of my comrades were killed within a very short time. Feng left me for dead, and the best resources and technology available to the military at the time were used to save my body and soul. So, here I am."

"It sounds like the most appalling experience. Is that how you got that large scar on your face?"

Merisi ran his fingers over the old, V-shaped injury.

"No, that was acquired much later—or earlier, depending on how you look at it." Merisi was mildly amused by the confusion that appeared on Richards' face. "A slight misadventure in the ninth century, Dottore, but let's not go there!

"Yes, I assume that my brush with Feng must have been very traumatic. I don't remember anything. What traces of memory of the incident and the subsequent treatment remained within me were erased. I am sure that it was the right thing for them to do, but unfortunately all memories of the early part of my life were lost as well. The very earliest event that I can recall is arriving at the military base for the first time. I must have been about eleven years of age. Of course, everything that I have told you about myself and my early development relates to my *official history*, but I have no actual memories of when I was very young. Sometimes I reflect on how convenient that must be for the people who put me back together . . . but there is nothing that I can do about that."

Richards felt compassion for the stranger. He was, of course, intimately acquainted with the concept of loss, but he could not imagine how it might feel to have no memories of his parents. He wondered whether his very painful childhood memories might be better than having no memories at all.

"It sounds like you have had your childhood stolen from you. Do you know anything about either of your parents?" he asked.

"Maybe," replied Merisi. "I have photographs of people who are allegedly my parents, along with two younger sisters, but there is little physical resemblance between them and me, and it is very difficult to believe anything that I have been told. Besides, that was all a long time ago now. I am what I am. An asset of the UNA. A human, but one that has been enhanced to the nth degree."

"And still the *property* of your military?"

"In a sense, everybody is the property of the military, as you put it. But yes. It's true that I have more human DPGM than Shui Feng. But when it comes down to it, I am as much an instrument of what's left of 'the state' as he is a weapon to be used by his creators. Although at least I am sure, deep down in my soul, that what I have done in my long career is for something that it righteous. Feng simply does not have a soul, however good he is at impersonating a human being. He is quite a celebrity, you know. In my time, they have what you know as cage fights between androids and enhanced humans. Feng is just about the best there is in that particular sphere. That sort of vice has existed in one form or another in every era I have experienced."

One minor detail of what Merisi said intrigued Richards the most.

"DPGM?" he asked.

"Ah! You will not know about DPGM. Are you familiar with DNA?"

"Yes, of course."

"Well, DPGM is the hereditary control mechanism that regulates the production of DNA and determines the information that is passed on to each organism's future generations—but you did not hear that from me!"

"So, with all this power and knowledge, and the ability to actually manufacture humans—" began Richards.

"Yes, there was a great deal of power derived from mankind's accumulated knowledge," interrupted Merisi. "But, increasingly, the product of all this knowledge was the ability to destroy, and to dominate, and to manipulate. Wisdom and an appreciation of the importance of cooperation and coexistence became all but lost.

"That is why my time spent with Merisi, who you know as Caravaggio, was such a revelation. Believe me—if you want to learn anything about the human condition and of the nature of our existence, then look to your past. It is to the likes of Shakespeare and Caravaggio that you must turn, and in your case, Dottore Richards, I am sure that this is what you need in order to complete your work and fulfil your potential. But there is another individual born just over two thousand years ago who had a more profound impact on the history of the world than any other!"

"You are referring to one Jesus Christ," Richards said.

"Exactly!" said Merisi with a raised finger. "And, in spite of your atheism, Dr. Richards, you accept that Christ was a man who lived, and whose life had a massive impact on history, do you not?"

Richards wondered why this stranger thought that he knew so much about him but decided not to deny being an atheist.

"I suppose I accept that he once lived," Richards conceded. "But he had a maximum of one life!" he added, raising a finger in a way that mimicked Merisi's gesture.

"So, do you not find it odd that this great man has no tomb, no burial place, not even an alleged place of burial?" asked Merisi. "And what do you make of the accounts of Christ's resurrection?"

Merisi lowered himself into an armchair, anticipating Richards' next question.

"Are you seriously suggesting that Christ was a time traveller, and that he disappeared into the future?"

"Travelled *to*. . . Travelled *from* . . ." Merisi smiled. "I have already revealed more than I am permitted to share, although when it comes to Jesus Christ people tend to believe what they want, so it doesn't really matter, I suppose. But what *is* important is that you realise that the early Christians knew a great deal about the secret of time travel."

"The *secret* of time travel?" huffed Richards.

"Yes, and that is exactly what it was—a secret it was their sacred duty to keep. And a secret that was kept for two and a half thousand years. Knowledge of the time portals, which were located throughout the Christian lands bordering the Mediterranean Sea, was entrusted to very few, and was never committed to tablet or parchment. Beyond Europe, the secret of the portals was guarded by holy men and women of other faiths. Over decades and centuries, great monuments, churches and other holy places were built over the portals. At first, the quest in Europe was to hide the portals from the Roman oppressors, but their location has also remained beyond the reach and imagination of adventurers and archaeologists. One of the portals, which is in fact not far from here, became buried under several tons of volcanic lava.

"So, you see, the combination of Christian diligence in keeping the possibility of time travel far from the sight of the world, and the blindness and lack of imagination of generations of scientists, succeeded in preserving the myth of the impossible for so long."

"And you're telling me that these portals exist today?" asked Richards.

"There are portals everywhere, gateways that allow those who have eyes to see to cross between worlds."

"And what has this got to do with me?"

"Dr. Richards, there are people from my world whose motives are corrupt and who mean to prevent you from developing your ideas. I have reason to believe, Dr. Richards, that they want to kill you!"

"Why me? And what makes you so sure?"

"Because they have done it already!"

Merisi paused to allow the enormity of what he had just said sink in. He studied Richards closely, and could see from the questioning expression on the young man's face that he was far from convinced about what he was hearing.

"Well, I feel very much alive now," began Richards, slowly, "so you must be trying to tell me that my death is somehow inevitable and unavoidable."

"Not unavoidable, or at least I hope not. But you were certainly assassinated—in fact, this very week. At the time, it was not something that drew a tremendous amount of attention—no offence, Dottore! But as we have since deduced from the study of the history of the twenty-first century, it is an event that changed the way in which energy was produced. And that is why I am here. My mission is to prevent your death."

Richards returned Merisi's fixed gaze. It was clear that the stranger was sincere. Yet the whole thing seemed fantastic. Utterly unbelievable.

Merisi didn't have to wait long for the inevitable volley of questions.

"You will appreciate that this is so much for me to take in," explained Richards.

"Of course."

"So, tell me. When is my assassination supposed to take place? Where? How? And by whom?"

"We do not have a complete picture," admitted Merisi, "but we know that you died here, in Milan, about three weeks after collapsing shortly after the seminar. An *open verdict* was recorded at your postmortem, Dottore, but according to what we have been able to deduce, you will have been poisoned with polonium-210, or a chemical very similar to that. Whoever wanted you dead must have had some very powerful connections to be able to get their hands on such materials. It is not a pleasant way to die. Your death has been recorded as being in three weeks from now."

Richards looked aghast and felt lighted headed.

"Don't worry, Dottore. I am here to prevent that event from happening. This is my job. My function. The authorities of my time have sent me because I am the best at what I do. I have a great deal of experience with this sort of thing."

"You seem very confident," Richards murmured, clearly shaken. "Yet you tell me that you don't know who it is who is supposed to have killed me. And you appear not to know exactly when and how I am going to be killed."

"Yes, but I am a quick learner, Dr. Richards," said Merisi with a reassuring smile. "Whoever administered the poison was merely flesh and blood. I am sure that I will be able to deal with him—or her."

Richards remained unconvinced. "Do you at least know how the poison was administered, assuming that everything else you're telling me is true?"

"Again, we are unsure," replied Merisi. "There are many ways of getting the substance into your bloodstream. They might have spiked your drink, or your food, or they might have got close to you in order to pierce your skin in some way. The chemical might even have been administered as a spray that you breathed in."

"It seems like a very broad range of possibilities," exclaimed an exasperated Richards.

"That's true, but please understand that your cause of death was recorded as being *unexplained*. Our historical analysts have had very little to go on, and the historical record certainly does not contain details of what you had for breakfast on the day you were murdered, or of who you were with in the hours leading up to your poisoning. That is why I have been sent here. I have been gathering information and sending it back to our analysts living in 2112.

"Everything points to GIATCOM Corporation being responsible. Your death left the way clear for them to build a powerful industrial empire with the generation of nuclear power at its heart. It might be difficult for you to appreciate this, but this modest seminar taking place this week marked a major potential turning point in the history of the world. If implemented, your ideas relating to sustainable power generation would prevent GIATCOM's hundred-year-long domination of the energy sector."

Richards ran both hands through his hair.

"Well, it is very simple, then," he said after a moment's contemplation. "I simply don't turn up at the seminar. I send my apologies. I will say that I have gone down with a bout of food poisoning, which, if what you are telling me has any substance, would actually not be very far from the truth."

"Unfortunately, it is not that simple, Dottore," said Merisi. "My mission actually has two objectives. The first one is to prevent your assassination. The second is to ensure that you will have the opportunity to follow through with your ideas, and to gain the financial backing to bring those ideas to fruition. That is why it is vital that you make your speech at the seminar tomorrow."

Richards grimaced with unease and apprehension.

"In fact, Dottore," continued Merisi, "I need you to follow precisely the routine that you have planned for the seminar, and for the hours leading up to the event. Do not accept an invitation to any additional meetings, and do not cancel any that you have planned. It is important that you do precisely what you did originally. You will not see me, but I will be close by, ready to intervene at the right time."

"It would actually make me feel a great deal safer if I could have you next to me," said Richards, smiling nervously. He felt very vulnerable.

"I am afraid that will not be possible, Dottore."

"Why not?"

"Because the situation is considerably more complicated." Merisi tugged gently at his right ear, a gesture that betrayed his own discomfort. "You see, I am not the only advanced operative from the twenty-second century to have come here through a time portal."

Richards cocked his head in astonishment. "There are more of you?"

"Unfortunately, it is not only my organisation, the United Nations Authority, that has the capacity for time travel. GIATCOM itself has a similar capability. In fact, I am certain that one of their assets has come here to Italy. I saw him in Siena."

"An agent trained to the same level as you?" asked Richards.

"Actually, it's worse than that; it's Feng himself," admitted Merisi, reluctantly. "Whatever his precise orders, I am certain GIATCOM wants to prevent me from completing my mission, which is to prevent your assassination. If he sees me, then he will simply find another way of eliminating you. But first we need to deal with the incident at the seminar. We can then turn our attention to whatever it is that GIATCOM might have planned."

Richards stood, his legs wobbly, and strode over to the window of the apartment. He peered out onto the street below, careful to remain behind the curtain to avoid being seen.

"Are you sure that you can protect me?" he asked Merisi.

"Nothing is certain, but I have not failed yet. And I am definitely your best chance."

Richards said nothing as he continued to gaze out of the window.

"After all," continued Merisi, "I saved you in Florence, and I have been watching over you ever since."

The reminder of the incident at the Ponte Vecchio cast Richards' mind back to the strange dart, which was still in the pocket of the jacket draped over an armchair.

"So, that dart. Was it fired at me by someone from your time?"

"Yes, by a GIATCOM operative. But what I saw in Siena will be a different proposition altogether. I will certainly be watching out for *him* at the seminar!"

Merisi wanted to make sure that the young engineer was fully aware of the enormity of what was at stake. He removed the pair of sunglasses from his inside breast pocket and passed the instrument to Richards. Richards studied the heavy black frames and what looked like earpieces in the covers at the end of each temple, turning them carefully in his fingers. He frowned and was about to pass them back when Merisi spoke again.

"They are perfectly safe, Doctor."

Richards paused, squinting again at every hinge and screw, pad and arm, before gingerly placing them on the bridge of his nose.

Within a heartbeat the lenses turned into a wide-angled television screen with full surround sound in his ears. A picture emerged with the acronym *UNA* and a logo with a white owl on a navy-blue background. In the centre it read, *Top Secret*.

The next moment, the screen changed and a title emerged.

Briefing: Dr. Ben Richards.

"What's this?"

"You'll see."

As the words faded, a tall and elegant woman with greying hair appeared on the screen. She was dressed in a navy-blue uniform with the UNA logo on her chest.

"Dr. Richards," she began. "I am an aide to Milton Westcroft, the President of the United Nations Agency, and I have sent Merisi, the man who is with you now, on a special mission to ask for your help."

Richards frowned.

"To understand why, I must tell you our story," she said. "Our world turned to one source of power generation fifty years ago." Images of new, white-painted nuclear reactors appeared. "We gave a company called GIATCOM the responsibility for developing one-world nuclear power generation."

"I've seen this in my dreams!" Richards cried as a pyramid at the heart of a city emerged with the word *GIATCOM* emblazoned in neon lights at its summit.

"Hush!" Merisi insisted.

"But there was a terrible accident," said the woman as an image of a billowing mushroom cloud on a desert horizon appeared. "A landmass the size of your North America was wiped out, eradicating hundreds of towns and cities and vaporising millions of men, women and children."

Images of bleak, grey hinterlands began to appear. The iron remains of tall buildings rose into leaden skies heavy with fallout while ashen flakes drifted towards the dusty ground.

"Our world—or *your* world as we had known it—was ruined. GIATCOM vowed to make amends and undertook the clear-up operation, but in truth the effects in a radius of 1,500 miles from the hypocentre were perpetually toxic, and the harm to people's health all over our world was unquantifiable."

Children appeared in front of his eyes, some newborn, others older, all suffering every imaginable deformity. Richards wanted to close his eyes to all the livid sores and staring faces, but he could not.

The camera returned to the president's aide. She was now sitting in a boardroom surrounded by vast windows looking out onto a granite sky. Sombre men and women in grey uniforms sat around the table.

"We have sent Merisi to find you and to ask for your help," she said. "We know that what you are championing is not being heard or received well in your time. But in ours we recognise that it is the only way we can guarantee the survival of our planet and of our people."

She pointed to a screen on the wall behind her, which ran an animation of extraordinarily tall buildings standing like the legs of a quadruped, their summits joined by girders that were now being covered by a curved roof.

As a roof formed atop each quartet of cloud-scrapers, Richards saw turbines lined up at the edges. They all began to spin as lights flickered on in every window below.

"We know that your design is ahead of its time," said the woman. "And we also know that your world has been through great economic hardship and that you cannot find funding for your project."

Too bloody right, Richards thought.

"If you choose to accompany Merisi to help us, we will provide you with all the resources you need to complete the project in your world as well as ours."

The woman paused as she looked down at a large, paper-thin tablet on the glass table in front of her. She picked it up and the screen immediately switched on.

Richards could see the words *Classified. Dr. Ben Richards.*

"We do not know the details of your ideas for innovation," she continued, "but we are sure that you alone in your world and ours know the correct design and material for these roof structures to harness a resource that will never run out and never fail us."

Richards let the faintest trace of a smile escape.

She said, "If you accompany Merisi, you will help us to save our world, and we can help you to save yours." Before the lenses switched off she added, "We believe in you, Dr. Richards."

Richards removed the glasses as Merisi leaned forward.

"Dottore, in spite of your value to us, there are people from my world who want to do you harm, and as I said, I have been sent here not just to ask for your help, but to protect you."

"You already have," Richards said, shuffling uncomfortably in his seat, "when you stopped that dart."

"Yes, it was likely filled with a radioactive element that is currently unknown in your time, designed to kill you," said Merisi as he stood. Stretching out his hand, he took the sunglasses back and pocketed them. "Will you come with me?" he asked.

Richards put his head in his hands for a moment. "I saw some of this in a dream," he sighed, wiping his sweaty hands on his trousers.

Merisi reached down and placed his hand on Richards' shoulder.

"This is no dream, Doctor," he said. "This is as real as you and me."

Richards looked up. "But I must deliver my lecture tomorrow."

Merisi frowned. "Leonardo da Vinci was here in this great city."

"So?" Richards asked, thrown off by the non-sequitur.

"He saw things that others did not understand."

"You're not comparing my findings with *his*?" Richards laughed.

"There are three classes of people, or so Leonardo once said," Merisi replied. "Those who see, those who see when they are shown, and those who do not see. You are one of those rare people who can *see*, Dr. Richards."

"Let's hope that those who come tomorrow learn to see," Richards sighed, scanning the room for a bottle of his favourite whiskey.

"One day everybody will see," Merisi said. "But for now, it is a battle. Here," he said, stretching out his hand. "This is a key. Conceal it from everyone. You may need it someday."

Richards took what looked like a credit card, only smaller, from Merisi's hand. One side was white and shiny. On the other was a picture of a sator square.

"How do I use this?" Richards asked.

"Just remember to say your Pater Noster," Merisi replied.

"I'm not religious."

Merisi laughed.

"No, seriously, what is this?" insisted Richards.

"You'll see."

Merisi walked towards the door and turned back to Richards. "Take great care, Doctor. Tell nobody what I have shared with you, not even your lady friend."

Richards frowned.

"Promise me," Merisi urged.

Richards shivered beneath his bathrobe.

"All right, I promise."

Richards saw the man hesitate, then nod, his eyes glowing.

"One more thing," Merisi said. "I followed you all the way here to this apartment without you seeing me."

"My friend spotted you," Richards interrupted.

"Yes, but despite her exertions, she didn't lose me. I just made her think she had."

"So?"

"So, I'm always nearby, just as I was at the Arno, the Savoy and on the autostrada here. I will be like the Little Madonna on the duomo, always watching over you."

With that the man in the white suit was gone, as silently and swiftly as he had come.

Richards stumbled to the bedroom. His legs buckled again, and he fell headlong onto the mattress. After a moment his breathing steadied. The blood returned to his cheeks and the strength to his joints and muscles. He stood again, facing the wall above the bedstead, gazing into the futuristic cityscape in the Crali painting. For several minutes he studied every part of the picture, as if he really were looking through a window onto something no longer imagined, but real. Could the stranger really deliver him into that far-off world?

The sound of the front door startled him.

"I'm back!" Rossini announced, a bag of groceries rustling in her arms. "And I've brought you a bottle of whiskey."

Richards turned, and as he watched the beautiful journalist unloading her bags onto the table, he recalled the remarkable way in which she caught his glass as it fell to the ground in the hotel restaurant that morning.

CHAPTER 13

ORDERS FROM GIATCOM

The door to the small office exploded open with a blinding flash of white light. Shui Feng had set the explosion to be as silent as possible to minimise the attention that it would attract in the dimly lit street outside. But he had not realised that the heat from the blast would set off the bookshop's fire alarm and sprinkler system.

The water from the sprinklers cleared the clouds of dust from the blast, enabling Feng to survey the devastation in the little bookshop nestled in a side street in the medieval centre of Siena.

Feng marched to the front door of the shop, neither pausing as he stepped over the body of the bookshop owner nor noticing that the carpet near the door had become soggy with blood from the fatal head wound he had inflicted on the man's wife. Feng quickly summed up the situation. The motorcycle he heard arrive at the shop had now disappeared, and it was clear that Merisi was not lying in wait for him—and Merisi had several minutes' start on him, so it would be pointless to try to pursue him.

Returning to the back room where he had left his Ducati, Feng activated his GIATCOM headset, and once again the eyepiece swung into position.

"Do you have news for me, Feng? Have you reached your location?" demanded a man in Feng's earpiece.

"Affirmative, but I am not the only one to have arrived."

"Merisi?"

"Affirmative. Merisi."

"I thought as much. I sent two androids through the Florence portal a few hours ago and they have failed to check in. That portal has now been closed from the inside. Only Merisi could have done that."

"So that was my backup team?"

"I'm afraid so. It was also Plan A, and two-thirds of my annual budget," added the man ruefully.

"Fuck your budget, Cardus!" snapped Feng. "You promised me backup, so send replacements!"

"Yes, yes. I will sort something out, but we can no longer use the Florence route."

"And Siena is no longer safe. Merisi must have followed me from the portal at the cathedral."

"Then it will have to be Capestrano. That's the next nearest. Have you secured your transport?"

"Affirmative."

"And is the rest of the equipment there and in order?"

"Maybe, but I cannot stay here any longer. There's a fire alarm ringing, and there are people starting to gather outside the shop. I need to get on my bike and leave."

"Okay. You will just have to improvise," Cardus sighed.

"I have already done that—twice," Feng said with a smirk as he glanced back into the main area of the shop, where the two innocent bodies lay.

"I do not wish to know the details. Just make sure that you destroy any equipment that you cannot take with you. Be at the Capestrano portal at eighteen hours today. A team will be there to meet you."

Feng removed the headset and stashed it neatly in his tunic pocket. The sound of voices grew louder as the shop door onto the street opened. Feng leaned against the heavy bookcase that had served as the secret door to the back room of the shop for some fifty years, and sealed the entrance just as he heard a succession of hysterical screams from a woman who had obviously just discovered the results of Shui Feng's improvisation.

Feng donned a black helmet and pressed the starter button of his black steed. After leaping astride the bike, he pressed the button on a device hidden in a small pocket inside his tunic, and a garage door at the back of the small room flipped up and over, allowing the mild night air to flood into the dark and cramped space. Feng paddled the bike outside into a small courtyard that led to a narrow, cobbled alley with a shallow gully running along its centre. As he turned the machine to follow the alley south, he took a small, oval object from his right boot and tossed it into the back room.

Feng had made his way to the end of the alley and was about to accelerate into a piazza when the incendiary device exploded some fifty yards behind him. This time, there had been no subtlety in the planning of the explosion, and he rode away with the entire bookshop and neighbouring properties ablaze. As he joined the unlit dual carriageway that led to the autostrada, Feng focused solely on his next objective—a rendezvous at the Abbey of St. Peter ad Oratorium, in the village of Capestrano some 200 miles to the south. The carriageway was empty and silent as dawn was about to break. His bike appeared to glide through the still air. He leaned forward with a sense of purpose. The growl from his engine echoed down the autostrada as the machine accelerated into the distance.

• •

After a three-and-a-half-hour ride, Feng saw Capestrano perched at the top of a hill, surrounded by rugged countryside filled with the dark-green hue of olive trees and vines. His eyes were drawn to the Castello Piccolomini, which dominated the site. Strategically located, the castle looked out upon the entire hilly region. But he was destined for the Benedictine Abbey of St. Peter ad Oratorium, on the banks of the Tirino River.

It had been a long, hot journey, with the summer sun beating down on his crash helmet for most of it. By the time he halted the Ducati by the riverbank, he was weary and saddle sore, and droplets of salty sweat irritated his eyes. He dismounted and removed his headgear, wiping the perspiration with a sleeve and observing for a moment the wet stain on the black leather. He then drew a white handkerchief from a jacket pocket and dabbed his eyes.

Through the burgeoning foliage, he could now make out the chalky walls of a large building standing in an enclosure at the centre of a clump of olive-green trees. Positioning his headset on the bridge of his nose, he homed in on the building.

Destination located, the lenses read. *San Pietro Ad Oratorium. 200 metres.*

Satisfied that he was in the correct location, Feng removed the headset and his all-leather black jacket. He stretched his arms out in both directions before dropping to the ground and performing press-ups. After several more lumbar exercises, he walked towards the fast-flowing water of the Tirino and knelt. Bowing as if in veneration, he scooped small handfuls of clear liquid from just above the gravel, keeping his eyes trained on his surroundings and his ears tuned to every sound.

Having slaked his thirst and cleansed his face, he returned to the dusty Ducati. He lifted his left hand to his face and directed his thoughts at a watch-like object on his wrist.

Destination acquired. Agent's ETA required.

Within a second, Feng had his answer as a hologram of a man in a white uniform with a GIATCOM logo appeared.

"Incoming, eighteen-thirty hours," the man said.

Feng stared at the image and channelled his thoughts: *Request latest mission parameters.*

"Infiltrate location for the target's lecture tomorrow," the GIATCOM official said. "Record target's address in full and relay to control for analysis."

Feng focused once again on the man. *What about the agents?*

"We are sending two simulants, briefed to masquerade as scientists attending tomorrow's event," the man replied.

And the target's abduction?

"Await further orders."

Feng hit a switch on the side of the watch and lowered his hand. Retrieving his helmet, he mounted the bike and fired up the engine.

He rode down a track between poplar trees until he reached an open gate. He turned off the engine, dismounted and wheeled the machine quietly down a gravelly path. Within minutes, he had arrived at a large open space with lush grass separating stony pathways. He approached the unmistakable Romanesque contours of San Pietro ad Oratorium, with its pasty walls and coral tiles. Feng leaned the motorcycle against a wall that was shaded beneath some lowering branches, covering it with their dense foliage, and made his way towards the church.

The front door indicated the centre of the church's simple facade, surmounted by a double arch of irregular stone engraved with palm trees in symmetrical patterns. Feng grasped one of two handles. The iron-studded door opened, and he stepped onto the ancient flagstones. Light flooded in behind him.

He closed the heavy door and walked down the empty nave, his steps dimly illuminated by the weak light intruding through the single lancet windows in front of him and the rectangular apertures to his left and right. The cool, sobering air refreshed him.

Passing seven arcades, each supported by pillars, he made his way down the centre aisle towards the presbytery, where an unadorned altar stood three steps above the main floor of the church, beneath a stone canopy supported by four columns. He raised his eyes above the capitals to a lunette where he made out the faded image of Saint Peter, the gatekeeper of heaven. He lowered his eyes and squinted as light poured in through a loophole window in the second of three apses behind the altar. He ignored the motes of dust that swirled in the air under the wooden trussed ceiling before disturbing the sombre silence of the sanctuary with the purposeful tread of his black boots.

Shui Feng turned towards an arcade on his left. There, carved on the wall of the north side of the church, was the telltale palindrome—five Latin words made up of five letters, each of which could be read from right to left, left to right, top to bottom and bottom to top:

ROTAS
OPERA
TENET
AREPO
SATOR

They were engraved in the exact reverse of their normal order.

Feng smiled as he approached the wall. Once again, he activated the communication device from his pocket, eyes fixed on the illuminated screen.

In position: Capestrano portal

Within seconds, the stone with the inverted sator square began to tremble with a blue light. Feng took several steps back towards the stone altar directly behind him.

The first simulant—a man about six feet tall—appeared in front of him, his head lowered as he entered through the north wall of the church. He moved to one side and was joined by a second machine, this time the manifestation of a woman of about thirty. The new arrivals were dressed in grey business suits and black, glossy shoes. Both had dark hair and incisive eyes.

Feng bowed his head, and they returned the gesture in mechanised unison. He peered into their inky retinas, transmitting his thoughts: *Latest orders from control.*

The simulants spoke immediately, their words reverberating around the north side of the church in a soulless litany.

"Control orders: travel to Milan. Neutralise target scientists tonight. Assume their identities. Enter Museum of Science and Technology eleven hours tomorrow. Attend lecture and await orders from Shui Feng."

Good.

Feng lifted the communication device to his face. He gazed into its tiny window and transmitted his thoughts once again.

Transmit profile.

An image of a well-built man appeared on the screen of the communicator. It downloaded simultaneously on the lenses of the dark eyepieces that had emerged from behind the right ears of both simulants and dropped down over their right eyes. The digital display relayed data wirelessly from Feng to the agents.

Mission Target: Doctor Benjamin Richards.
Age: 32.
Nationality: British
Occupation: Lecturer in Engineering.
Expertise: Wind turbine technology.
Height: 1.87m.
Weight: 90kgs.
Hair: Blonde.
Eyes: Blue.
Status: Single.
Strengths: Innovation, industry, ingenuity.
Weaknesses: Fear of not being believed, interpersonal skills.
Asset status: Level 5 asset.
IQ: Creative Genius.
Mission parameters: Abduction only.

Feng replaced the transmitter in his pocket, and the simulants' eyepieces retracted. *Come this way*, he told them.

Feng headed towards the main door. Passing the seven arcades on each side, he donned his sunglasses. He pushed against the door, and a brilliant light drenched the three visitors as they stepped out from the cool and musty sanctuary into the late-afternoon sunshine. The garden fragrances invaded Feng's senses as he inhaled the warm air.

Reconnaissance, he determined. The lenses on his sunglasses transitioned into search mode as he scanned the locality in a 360-degree movement. The simulants imitated his movement exactly, their darkened eyepieces having deployed once again. The only thermal shape discerned by their infrared vision was a rabbit scurrying into its warren some thirty metres away.

Follow me. Feng marched from the right-hand side of the church and scaled a low wall. His companions jumped it in a simultaneous, athletic movement.

He shimmied through small bushes and hurdled over untended plants for fifty metres, heading towards the Tirino

River. Ten metres from its banks, Feng took a sudden left towards a cluster of impenetrable shrubs and trees. He raised his wrist device, activating a switch on its side. He pointed the device at the thicket, and immediately two heavily laden branches above the knot of trees began to move like arms, revealing an arched canopy and creating a doorway into a sun-dappled grove.

The three visitors crossed the threshold, and the leafy gateway closed behind them.

Feng pointed left with his device. The drooping limbs of the saplings and trees moved upwards and outwards, unveiling a wooden shack on the left side of the dishevelled grotto. Feng went to the shack's door and pointed the face of his device towards it. A hissing sound, incongruous in such a rustic hollow, indicated that the lock had been disabled.

The door opened towards him, snapping the clinging branches and creepers. Refracted rays of sunlight streaming through the branches above bathed the interior of the hidden shelter. Inside were four large objects under cobwebbed tarpaulins and a collection of carefully stacked boxes and crates along three walls. Shui Feng removed one of the canvas covers, revealing a red Ducati that was otherwise a replica of his own black vehicle— same design, same badges and markings. He then uncovered a second, identical machine. Feng walked into the recesses of the shack. He opened a parcel-sized container on top of some boxes and withdrew a wallet, a purse and several keys.

He gave one key to the male simulant, and then withdrew a driving licence and a photo ID from the bulging pockets of the wallet, all meticulously designed to reflect the period in which they were travelling. He checked the documentation carefully before handing it to the simulants. They walked past Feng into the chamber and wheeled the red motorcycles out of the hut. Feng retrieved two helmets and closed the door, moving shrubs and branches to conceal the opening. He then walked away and used his device to reinstate the arboreal canopy over the shack. He turned to the simulants.

I will be in a concealed location in the Museum of Science and Technology in Milan when you rendezvous there tomorrow at eleven hours, he said. *Locate your targets and assume their identity; do not—I repeat, do not—kill them. There can be no timeline violations.*

The shape-shifting simulants returned an invisible message of confirmation.

There is a track outside, leading back to the road along the banks of the river. Use that.

Feng then shifted from telepathic to voice communications.

"From now on, particularly in the presence of people, we will communicate verbally. Let your plans be as dark and impenetrable as the night. And when you move, fall like a thunderbolt."

Feng bowed before opening up the grotto. The simulants mounted their vehicles and fired up the engines before manoeuvring cautiously past him. Veering to the right, they hastened along the distinct but untrodden trail as the arms of the trees folded behind them.

Shui Feng raised the device on his wrist.

Rendezvous successful. Agents dispatched to Milan. Heading to target destination now.

He then ran swiftly from the grotto, retracing his steps to Saint Peter's church, and made his way to the well-camouflaged, black machine. As he prepared to ignite the engine, he turned back towards the church, its pasty walls clearly visible through the gaps in the trees. Three men dressed in black cassocks were approaching the door of the church. The two at the rear wore dog collars and black birettas. The man at the front was bare-headed and clearly a layman. He held a single-chain thurible. Smoke from burning incense billowed through perforations in the silver censer, rising into the sky with the thurible's three double swings.

As the three men entered the church, they chanted in Latin: "*Adore te devote, latens Deitas, quae sub his figures verelatitas* . . ."

The translation appeared immediately inside Feng's visor: *I adore you, O hidden God, truly concealed beneath these bare shadows . . .*

Passing over the threshold, their voices faded, along with the final wisps of white smoke. Feng closed the visor on his helmet.

Destination: Milan. Museum of Science and Technology.

And with that, the black Ducati sprang into life.

CHAPTER 14

ADVICE FROM AN OLD FRIEND

"I'm just heading out for a walk!" Richards shouted as he draped a slate-grey sweater over his shoulders.

"I'll come with you if you wait," Rossini answered from the bedroom.

"Thanks, but I need some alone time to get my head in gear for my lecture tomorrow," Richards said. "I'll not be long."

Richards headed for the door of the apartment and within minutes was walking up a street made damp by a recent gentle shower.

He removed his smartphone and reviewed the most recent conversation under the heading *Padre Giovanni, Milan Cathedral*. He selected the number and soon heard a familiar voice.

"Father Luigi, how are you, my old friend? I have arrived in Milan for my lecture tomorrow at the Museum of Science and Technology. May I see you this evening?"

"Ben! Of course! It would be a pleasure. I am pleased that you are here in the city. How about nine at the cathedral? Ask an usher for me."

"I look forward to it."

"I would like a ticket to your lecture!"

"Of course! I will bring a ticket with me. See you later, Father. Ciao!"

Richards smiled as he placed the phone back in his jacket pocket. Father Luigi had been a very close friend of Richards' father. When Richards was orphaned, the priest took the young boy under his wing. Richards lived in a succession of foster homes, and Father Luigi was the one constant presence in the young man's life; he was like a benevolent uncle.

Richards always felt guilty about not staying in touch with the priest as often as he should and was delighted to spend time with someone who had provided so much support when he needed it the most.

Richards strolled through the suburban neighbourhood, keeping a watchful eye out for suspicious men on fast motorcycles and never straying far from the apartment. He returned to find Rossini sitting at a wooden table in the kitchen. She stood as he approached, and he noticed her anxious expression.

"What's up?"

"I just had a call from my boss. I'm sorry, but he wants an article from me by this evening to go to press tomorrow. And I wanted to be able to relax this evening."

"That's a shame," replied Richards. "There was someone that I wanted to introduce you to—someone very special to me."

Rossini listened intently as Richards told her about the unlikely relationship that developed between the Italian priest and the orphaned boy from England. She was fascinated to learn more about the man that she had known for just a few days but with whom she was becoming more and more intrigued. She felt rather awestruck by Richards' intellect and found his ambitious energy and drive intoxicating. But her sharp and perceptive journalist's mind detected a vulnerability.

"Well, I am sure that you will have a great deal to talk about this evening," she said. "I imagine that you don't get many opportunities to meet."

"That's true. But I don't communicate with him as often as I should. There was a time when he was like a father to me. But I have never really returned the affection that he deserves."

"Then it's good that you'll have the opportunity to spend some time with him this evening."

"Yes, and I would like to pick his brains about one or two things," said Richards. "He might have some ideas about what's been happening to me lately."

Grazia wasn't sure what Ben was referring to, but time was pressing for them both, so she changed the subject to the issue of what they were going to eat that evening. They agreed that there was only time for a snack, and together they busied themselves preparing a meal using the baguettes, butter and cheese that Rossini had bought earlier that day, adding herbs they found in the kitchen.

"Tell me more about this little boy from the northeast. How did you end up spending so much time with an Italian priest when you were young? Where was your mother? And what was she like?"

"Oh, my mother was a singer—a great singer!" he said with a proud smile, deliberately avoiding answering the full question.

"Ah, that's where you get your desire to perform from then?"

"Well, doesn't everyone want to be recognised?"

"Not everyone. They just want to be happy with their life in this fast-paced capitalist world we live in, Doctor."

"And what about you?" asked Richards, diverting the conversation away from himself. "Have you ever had the urge to perform in front of people?"

"I suppose so. I was an athlete. I was the under-seventeens fifteen-hundred-metre champion, which helped me in my training as a special agent for the undercover police. That was before I decided on journalism as a career."

"Ah!" Richards smiled. "That answers a few of my questions."

• •

Shortly before eight thirty that evening, after reminding Rossini to double-lock the door after he had left and promising to not return too late, Richards set off from the parking area of the plush apartment block in the western suburbs, heading for the Duomo di Milano in the centre of the city. Twenty minutes later, he parked the rented vehicle in the Autosilo Diaz in the Piazza Armando Diaz and strode through a bustling night market.

At the cathedral piazza he headed towards the enormous, pallid facade of the duomo—one of the largest Gothic edifices in Italy and the world. As an engineer, Richards appreciated the angular structure of the vast, imposing building, marvelling at the detail of the ornate decoration. However, he was distracted by a large banner draped across the entrance of the building. It read, *'For **God** so loved **the** world, that he **gave his only Son**, that whoever believes in him should not perish but **have eternal life.' John 3:16***

Inside, there were columns and statues everywhere, with the most elaborate carvings and designs. Straight ahead of him, an altar was bathed in a sublime light, creating a chiaroscuro in which three priests celebrated Mass with an almost mechanical efficiency. Ancient Latin chants lingered like incense as Richards passed statues and sarcophagi, searching for an usher. It wasn't long before he spotted a tall, bespectacled youth helping visitors to light prayer candles, then place them among row upon row of blazing lights, as many as the spires adorning the roof and walls of the cathedral.

As Richards approached, the priestly chants were replaced by a modern, cacophonous toccata from an unseen organist. Nearing the usher, the smell of polished wood from the ranks of pews yielded to a fusion of burning candle wax and frankincense.

"Excuse me," Richards said to the young cassocked layman. "My name is Dr. Ben Richards, and I'm here to see Padre Luigi at nine."

The lanky usher nodded and beckoned him to follow. They walked over a marble floor adorned by a mosaic of black, white and red squares decorated with floral patterns. They then descended under the main altar to the crypt, entering a small room in which an ornate chandelier illuminated a martyr's sarcophagus. The usher knocked on a door to the right of the saint's opulent grave.

"Enter," a man called from within.

The usher opened the door.

"Ah, Ben!" he said. "How wonderful to see you again!"

A short, plump priest with silver spectacles advanced from behind a mahogany desk. He smiled and proffered his hand.

"I am so glad that you could come! It's your first time visiting the duomo?"

"It is," Richards said as the usher left.

"Then that is all the more reason why it is good that you are here. It is impressive, no?"

"Very."

"Mark Twain, he said it was an anthem sung in stone, a poem wrought in marble."

"He had a way with words."

The priest laughed. "He said it was greater than Saint Peter's in Rome."

Richards smiled.

"Please, sit."

Richards plunged into a mahogany chair with armrests in front of the desk.

"So, what have you been up to in Italy? Have you come direct to Milan from London?"

Richards told the priest about the time that he had spent in Florence but decided not to alarm the priest by mentioning the incident with the dart near the Ponte Vecchio. He also chatted freely and fondly about the girl he had just met, not disclosing his attraction to her. He had not forgotten that Father Luigi was a man of fairly conservative principles, and they had rarely discussed affairs of the heart—let alone the flesh—during his youth. Young Ben didn't make time for girls. Instead, he was absorbed in his studies and his research. The priest encouraged Richards' proclivity, knowing the sudden death of the boy's parents meant Ben Richards would have to be self-made and self-sufficient. The boy's single-mindedness reminded the priest of his own life, having dedicated himself to the church from the age of fifteen.

The pair chatted for more than an hour, reminiscing over old times, with Richards patiently responding to a litany of questions about his life and his plans. Richards pulled out his wallet. He withdrew a business card on which he had drafted the curious word square that appeared on the key Merisi gave him. He felt it was best to heed the stranger's warning not to reveal the key itself, but the palindromic arrangement of the letters fascinated him. Their symmetry appealed to Richards' organised mind; he suspected that the square might have a deeper meaning. He considered Father Luigi to be the wisest and most widely read man he had ever known, and so he presented the card to him, faceup on the ink blotter in front of the priest, and scrutinised the old man's face for a reaction.

"Have you ever seen one of these before, Father?" he asked.

The priest lifted the card to his oval lenses and peered closely at the letters, but he had immediately recognised what was drafted on the card.

"This is a sator square," he said.

"What is that, exactly?"

"It is an ancient Christian code. Several have been found on the premises, or in the ruins of churches throughout Europe. Typically, the squares are found engraved in stone or clay."

"Are you sure it's Christian?" Richards asked.

"Why do you doubt it?"

"Well, as the words in the square appear to be Latin, isn't there a chance that it is a design that pre-dates Christianity?"

"Well, the oldest sator square ever found was in the city of Pompeii."

"And Pompeii was destroyed in AD 79. Christ died in AD 33, or thereabouts, so is it feasible that a church with one of these squares carved on it could have been built there in such a short time?"

"That depends on what you mean by *church*," the priest said. "Perhaps you do not know that there were no church buildings to speak of between our Lord's resurrection in approximately AD 33 and the time of Emperor Constantine three hundred years later. And not all of the sator squares have been found embedded in the walls of holy buildings. It is true that there is a sator square on one wall of the Duomo di Siena, but others have been found on stone tablets. Besides, the early Christians gathered in simple homes in cities all over the Roman Empire."

"You mean they were like house churches?" Richards asked.

"They were not *like* house churches," the priest said. "They *were* house churches. The first Christians met in peoples' homes. They very often had to."

"Why?"

"It was too dangerous to meet in public. They were violently persecuted. Two thousand years ago it cost people everything to follow Christ. The emperor in Rome was the most powerful man in the world, and he was worshipped with the titles *son of god* and *saviour*. Of course, these were the titles the first Christians gave to Jesus. That was political dynamite. The Roman Empire began to hate them because they were suggesting that Jesus was Lord—and Caesar was not."

"What happened?"

"They were forced into making a choice," the priest sighed. "Once every year, on the emperor's birthday, every man and woman in the empire was ordered to head to the nearest amphitheatre to burn incense."

"Catholics burn incense," Richards protested.

"Yes, but we do not have to make an idolatrous confession at the same time—that Caesar is *dominus et deus*, Lord and God."

Richards frowned. "I see."

"Those who refused were bankrupted, exiled or killed in the most horrible ways," the priest continued, "and the result was that the church—the extended families of Christ's brothers and sisters—started to meet in secret, behind closed doors, in people's homes."

"Do you think this happened in Pompeii?"

"We know it did."

The priest stood and walked to a bookcase and lifted a huge leather-bound volume sitting on its side on a bottom shelf. He opened it and turned the pages.

"Here," he said, placing the book on the desk and pointing to some graffiti on an ancient, damaged stone in a black-and-white photograph.

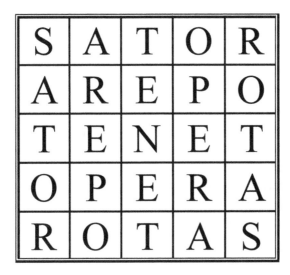

"A sator square!" Richards exclaimed.

"It was found in Pompeii on a doorjamb in the entrance of the house of a baker named Proculo."

"But there's no evidence that it's Christian."

The priest turned a page. "Here's the proof," he said.

Richards leaned forward as the priest directed the head of a desk lamp to provide more light. There was another old photograph, this one showing an engraving of a fish right above a sator square.

"We both know the extent to which I failed to teach you to be a good Christian, Ben, but even you will know the symbolic significance of the fish."

"Of course. The fish is an ancient code for Christianity," replied Richards.

"Yes. In Greek—the main language of the day—the word for fish is *icthus*. These letters form an acrostic: *ICTHUS, Iesous Christos Theios Huios Soter*. It means 'Jesus Christ, Son of God, Saviour,' the very titles that the Romans hated."

"And how is this proof?"

"The fish and the square were also found in Pompeii."

Richards looked up into the priest's eyes. "So why are people so adamant that Christians weren't in Pompeii?"

"Perhaps because we live in a time when there are dark forces at work wanting to bury Christianity under the grey ash of secularism."

Richards took a deep breath and sat back in his chair. "So there really were Christians in Pompeii?"

"There were Christians in Rome twenty years before Vesuvius erupted."

"So?"

"So, Rome is only 150 miles from Pompeii, and with the excellent transport system created by the empire it would have been easy for Christians to travel there and begin a small house church in the doomed city. When Nero became emperor, they would have had to meet in hiding, hence the fish symbol and the sator square."

"You still haven't told me what the square means," Richards said.

"It doesn't mean anything."

"You're joking!" Richards cried.

"I am not. Here," the priest said, placing the white business card on top of the antiquarian book. "Look at these five words."

Richards pored over the drawing.

"They form a palindrome. Every which way you read these five words, they read the same."

"So, what's the translation?"

"There isn't one!"

"But that cannot be right!"

"Remember that the earliest Christians in Pompeii wanted their secret meeting places to be identified by their friends, but not their enemies. The sator square was a signal or a code. It concealed its meaning from unbelievers, while revealing its meaning to believers."

"But these are Latin words!" Richards protested.

"Yes, they are. *Sator* means 'the sower.' *Tenet* means 'holds.' *Opera* means 'works.' *Rotas* means 'wheels.'"

"You've left out *arepo*!"

"That doesn't mean anything," the priest chuckled. "The best that scholars can come up with is the theory that it is the name of the sower."

"It's like a first-century Rubik's cube," Richards laughed.

"Except that the solution was known only to a very few people," the priest said.

"And what is the solution?"

The priest took a blank sheet of white paper from a drawer in his desk and started to write in black ink, using an old fountain pen.

"These are the letters of the sator square, rearranged in a different order," he said.

<pre>
            P
            A
            T
            E
            R
P A T E R N O S T E R
            O
            S
            T
            E
            R
</pre>

"*Pater noster*!" Richards cried. "*Our Father*! The first words of the Lord's Prayer."

"Precisely! Well, I'm pleased that you remember at least something of what I taught you."

Richards ignored the good-humoured jibe.

Father Luigi had always been troubled by Richards' atheism, which had developed at a remarkably young age. But he respected the boy's right to hold his own convictions on religion. Much later in life, Richards concluded that they had both been rather bound in their thinking. He felt that his adherence to rationality and the scientific method served as a barrier to the priest's religious teachings. He was inclined to despise Father Luigi's apparently slavish devotion to the teachings of the Bible, dismissing it as being a prerequisite for the professional vocation the father had chosen. Upon reflection, he wished that they had both been a little more open-minded. Maybe that would have enabled them to have a closer personal relationship.

The engineer stared at the sheet of paper and then back at the drawing of the square.

"But you haven't used all the letters!"

"Bravo, Ben! You are right. There are two *As* and two *Os* that need to be added."

He adjusted his drawing, adding the missing letters to the ends of the cruciform shape.

```
                        A
                        P
                        A
                        T
                        E
                        R
  A  P  A  T  E  R  N  O  S  T  E  R  O
                        O
                        S
                        T
                        E
                        R
                        O
```

"In a way, that spoiled it," Richards sighed. "Those new letters look redundant."

"Not to a first-century Christian," the priest retorted.

"Why?"

"The letters *A* and *O* are far from redundant; they are sacred. They are the first and last letters of the Greek alphabet, *Alpha* and *Omega*. This is how the first Christians worshipped Christ—as the Alpha and the Omega, the *first* and the *last*, the *beginning* and the *end*."

Richards rubbed his chin. "So, you're saying the sator square is a code."

"Yes."

"And it functioned as a kind of key for those in the know?"

"Yes. Even today, you can see where they probably met. There is an atrium on the site of Pompeii, just opposite a brothel, named the Hotel of the Christians. It is a house with many rooms, suggesting that it was used for hospitality before the volcano erupted. On one wall, archaeologists in 1862 found an enigmatic graffito with the word *Christianos* on it."

"That is interesting," Richards said. "So, Christians in Pompeii would come to the atrium and see the sator square and know it was a safe house.

"If you had eyes to see," the priest said. "The *Our Father* opened the door onto another world."

"What world?"

The priest frowned, exasperated at his friend's apparent ignorance. "The kingdom of heaven on earth, of course," he said. "The world as it was always meant to be."

As soon as the priest uttered these words, a breeze entered the room. The lamplight flickered for a moment, and the letters on the white sheet shimmered in the intermittent glow.

The priest removed his glasses, closed his eyes and bowed his head. When he looked up again, his eyes glistened with tears.

"I don't know why you are so interested in sator squares, but if you ever feel the need to speak with me about this issue, or anything else to do with religion, you have my number."

"Yes, of course," Richards said.

"But for now, I really need to be getting home."

Both men stood and bade each other the fondest farewell.

"Thank you, Father," said Richards, reaching into his pocket and withdrawing an invitation card. "For the lecture tomorrow." He smiled.

"Thank you," the priest replied, returning the business card with the sator square.

Richards made for the door, but before he left the chamber he turned back to the priest.

"I have already presumed too much upon your time, Father, but I have one more question."

The priest smiled.

"Do you believe that there are portals that lead to parallel worlds?"

"Only one," the priest replied.

"Where is it?"

"Not *where—who*." The priest smiled again. "The one who said, 'I am the door.'" The priest lifted the heavy book from the desk. As he returned it to its shelf, he looked over his spectacles and said, "*Pax vobiscum,*" whereupon Richards crossed the threshold and took his leave.

CHAPTER 15

INFILTRATION

The two TX-series androids sped past the Piola metro station in Milan and pulled up beneath the twitching European flags of the three-storey Hotel Piola in the Via Alessandro. They checked the time on the communication devices strapped to their wrists before sending a message. The screens on both devices glowed phosphorescent blue.

02h00. Destination reached. Hotel Piola.

They wheeled their motorcycles a short distance down the street and parked them in a side alley. Then they both removed their helmets before striding up the street and behind the hotel. They scaled a whitewashed wall with swift, mechanical movements, and slid silently down into a small space behind some bushes at the far end of the hotel's simple garden. Peering through the foliage, they saw a veranda. Wine bottles and ashtrays littered the round, metal tables. All was deserted.

TX1 and TX2 checked their communicators once again. The same data had been fed, from a source that was far away in time and space, to both devices.

Targets located in Room 17, Second Floor: Tracking & Guidance initiated.

The simulants hauled themselves up onto a first-floor balcony. TX1 removed a device from his belt, which he held against the lock of the double doors in front of him. With a faint orange-red glow, the cylinder of the lock slid to one side. Silently, TX1 opened the door, and both intruders slipped through salmon-coloured curtains into the hotel dining room. Passing a bar, also salmon-pink, they paused before a door. Without hesitation, they activated a switch on their communicators.

Motion detectors activated.

The simulants tilted their heads at exactly the same angle at exactly the same moment. Nothing moved on the first floor of the building. They opened a glass door leading to the stairs and ascended to the second floor. Opening another glass door, they walked into a corridor. Following the glowing dot on TX1's tracker, they passed rooms 13 through 16 before arriving at their destination.

The female TX2 simulant stretched out a hand and extended her index finger to its full length. A thin, jagged blade the length and width of a Georgian meat skewer emerged and penetrated the lock. It noiselessly turned and the mechanism clicked.

The simulants tilted their head towards each other and then looked down at their wrists. A slight movement registered on the motion tracker. One of the occupants inside had briefly shifted in bed. The two intruders stood still, their hands by their sides as if standing at ease on a drill parade.

A few seconds later, they tilted their head towards each other again and then nodded. The female android silently opened the door, and soon the two androids were inside the room. TX1 scanned the room using the device on his wrist. The screen revealed a thermal image of two people sleeping side by side. The slumbering bodies were those of Volker Boer and Nadine Lester, a husband and wife who were senior lecturers in the Aeronautical Engineering Department of the University of Glasgow's School of Engineering.

Words appeared on the androids' devices. *Targets: Boer. Lester.*

TX1 made his way to the far side of the king-sized bed and waited. TX2 assumed her position on the other side. They both extended their right index fingers towards their targets. A tiny surgical needle deployed from both. The eyes of the simulants dilated as the needles extended at the same moment to the same length, a hair's width from the jugular vein on the side of each sleeper's neck. For a heartbeat, the needles lingered just above the skin before penetrating flesh and artery. Both sleepers stirred momentarily.

The woman sighed; the man groaned. Then they were still.

The simulants stepped back, each directing the screen of their communicators at the bed. A soft, blue light illuminated the sleepers. The man was identical in appearance to TX1, the male simulant. TX2 was identical to the female.

The two new doppelgangers went to work immediately and efficiently. TX1 picked up Volker Boer, a Dutchman of substantial build, as if his victim were a small dog, and wrapped the unconscious body in the light-green eiderdown. He bundled him into one side of a tall wardrobe, and then TX2 placed Nadine Lester next to him.

They then entered data into their communicator.

Targets neutralised until 16h00.

The androids turned to the bed, removed their clothes and slipped under the single cotton sheet. Their eyes remained open, but the light within went out.

• •

Shui Feng unpacked a small, grey, textile bag fastened at the top by a black drawstring. He had chosen the cramped, shabby toilet of a fairly seedy bar as a changing room. It was a disgusting facility, but accessible through a long, narrow flight of steps at the rear of the establishment, so he felt that there was little chance of him being disturbed.

Squatting on his haunches, Feng laid the contents out on the floor and selected from the array of gadgets an implement. The two-inch-long device resembled a miniature child's top from the Victorian era. He stood and pressed a button on top of the instrument, then passed it slowly from the top of his head to the soles of his feet. Within a second or two, his appearance had transformed. His close-cropped, military-style hair was now a long and silky raven black cascading from his shoulders. His lips were rouged, and dark makeup around his eyes emphasised the deep brown of his irises. In place of the functional, skin-tight outfit that he had worn as he entered the Bamboo Bar, he now wore a black dress made of fine velvet, which hugged the contours of a lithe, feminine body. The transformation was completed by a pair of black Gucci shoes with stiletto heels.

Feng glanced briefly in the cracked and dirty mirror hanging above a small, vandalised wash basin before collecting the remainder of his equipment and stashing it away in the small bag. He then made his way down the long flight of stairs, crossed the deserted street, and set off on the next stage of his mission.

CHAPTER 16

THE SEMINAR IN MILAN

INSTITUTO DI ENERGIA, MILAN, ITALY

Richards was overwhelmed by the challenge of affixing a name tag to his lapel.

"Are you struggling with that, Ben?" Grazia Rossini asked.

"No, I'm fine," the engineer lied.

"Here, let me do it for you," she insisted.

Within a second or two, the conference badge—green to denote that Ben Richards was a speaker—was in place.

"There!" She smiled.

The conference registration desk in the foyer had become crowded, with some thirty minutes remaining before Richards was due to start the afternoon's proceedings with a keynote speech. He was inspecting his badge to make sure it was pinned when a handsome young man with an immaculately trimmed beard approached and read the name tag.

"Aha! Dr. Ben Richards!" the man said with an unmistakeable English-public-school accent while chewing gum. "It seems that we are due to be on stage together!"

Richards was visibly shaken by the bold approach, so Rossini intervened. "And you are?"

"Rick Bryce-Fairbrother," he said, pointing to his name tag and extending a hand into Rossini's and then holding on while looking into her eyes. "I'm an economist. I sort of look after people's investments in energy companies."

Richards surmised that Bryce-Fairbrother enjoyed a high six-figure salary for managing wealthy client portfolios. In fact, Richards had come across him before at conferences. He had always despised the man, being secretly a little jealous of how at ease Bryce-Fairbrother was in front of an audience. Although he knew little of the man's background, Richards was naturally suspicious of this sort of person, assuming the wealth of one so young must inevitably be due to a privileged upbringing, an affluent post code and membership of the right sort of gentlemen's club. *It's who he knew and who he knows,* Richards thought. His jealousy flared again as the beautiful Italian journalist appeared to be intrigued by the dapper investor.

"And what sort of people do you work for?" Rossini asked.

"Oh, you know. The usual suspects. BP, npower, Elf, and one or two American companies." He proudly smiled.

Of course you do, thought Ben with an air of resignation.

"It keeps me out of trouble," quipped Bryce-Fairbrother.

"Oh, how interesting!" exclaimed Rossini. She was about to ask another question when Richards, appearing rather peeved, interrupted.

"I'm due to deliver the keynote speech in about half an hour. I'd better make myself known to the conference chairman. So, you are a panel member?"

"Yes," replied Bryce-Fairbrother, again pointing to his name tag. "I'm here express the point of view of investors, and to add some hard economic reality to the debate."

Ben steadied, trying not to react to the barbed remark obviously cast to roil him.

"Well, I'm confident that I have a sound business case for my ideas," he calmly retorted.

"Splendid! Well, I'll look forward to hearing all about it soon, then."

With that, Bryce-Fairbrother turned to Rossini, flashing his most charming smile, and sauntered off into the main hall of the auditorium.

"What an interesting young man," cooed Rossini like a smitten high school girl. "He's what we Italian girls think of as a typical Englishman."

"I suppose so," sniffed Richards. "Anyway, I'd better go and find the conference chairman."

• •

The conference chairman, Professor Alessandro Giuffrè, rose and stood near the edge of the stage. The murmur of conversation ceased. The grey-haired Italian, clad in a crumpled, beige tweed suit, read from a small printed card.

"I am very pleased to welcome our keynote speaker this evening, Dr. Ben Richards," he announced in a heavy English accent.

Ben Richards waited patiently as Giuffrè read the brief biography that Richards himself had prepared.

"The title of Dr. Richards' speech is *Experts' opinions of the innovative application of stadium roof mounted turbine array versus conventional large freestanding turbine generation*. Dr. Richards, the floor is yours."

As Richards strode to the lectern at the front of the stage, he caught the eye of Rossini sitting in the second row. She gave him a reassuring smile. He smiled back at her as he placed his lecture notes next to the microphone.

"Good afternoon!" he said, confidently and clearly, now focusing on the job in hand. He thanked the conference chairman for the introduction and made some rather banal remarks about how pleased he was to be in the city that was hosting the seminar—something that he had done many times. Presentations of this nature had become a matter of routine and, as usual, he glanced around the audience as he spoke.

Conscious of the revelations that had been made to him by Merisi the previous day, Richards surveyed the sea of faces with apprehension. After all, according to the mysterious, bearded stranger, today was to be the day of his assassination. Richards had never had an issue with sleeping, but after his conversation with Merisi, he had found himself lying awake in the early hours.

"You will notice," he continued, "that I am joined on the stage this afternoon by a collection of very eminent people who are all experts in their field." Very pleased to distract the audience's gaze from himself, Richards introduced each of the smartly suited panel members, which included one woman. Each was seated behind a long table covered with a dark-green, cotton cloth. Each nodded in acknowledgement when Richards mentioned their name.

The panel represented an impressive array of academic, commercial and economic expertise. They included, seated at the far end of the table, the academic couple Volker Boer and Nadine Lester, who watched proceedings with an air of silent detachment. The imposters were joined on the panel by a leading turbines research scientist, a wind engineer, an aerodynamics consultant, the director of a structural engineering firm, and Richard Bryce-Fairbrother, the economist.

"And," continued Richards, "we are missing one very important individual—Professor Albert Einstein!" There was a subdued chuckling throughout the audience.

Richards pressed on. "And so, we must satisfy ourselves with some of his best-known quotations. 'Imagination is the highest form of research.' 'Imagination is everything; it is the preview of life's coming attractions.' 'Knowledge is limited—imagination encircles the world.'

"This evening, I would like to explain to you the innovative concept of mounted, integrated wind turbines, also known as BUWTs. These are designed to be positioned in urban and semi-urban locations, on the roof of stadia such as the one we have here."

Richards drew the audience's attention to a representative scale model of a football stadium that was to form the centrepiece of his presentation. Complete with bespoke turbines mounted on the roof, it sat like a white wedding cake on a raised wooden table just to Richards' left.

"The advantage of a rooftop position such as this," he said, "is that it can utilise otherwise dormant space to generate renewable energy. Something that is central to my idea is the Coanda Effect, which is named after another genius, the Romanian scientist and pioneer Henri Coanda. This relates to the behaviour of gases and fluids and is the mechanism by which a stream of air sort of sticks itself to a flat roof as it passes over it.

"The Coanda Effect is easy to demonstrate in general terms—and most simply using the example of a stream of water falling vertically from a tap. If you place a convex object, such as the outside of a glass basin or a spoon, adjacent to this stream of water so that it is just in contact with it, the fluid will attach itself to that surface and bend around it for a considerable distance. If you dangle the spoon next to the stream of water in such a way that it is free to move in any direction, you will feel that it is drawn towards the falling water—rather like a magnet. The extent to which the water sticks to the object will depend upon the precise shape of that object."

From the pinched expressions from one or two members of the audience, Richards detected a slight air of scepticism, and so he hurried on to the paper-lift demonstration, a trick that Father Luigi had taught him after the priest detected a spark of interest in science and technology in the bright teenager.

"A stream of air—or a wind—behaves in exactly the same way as the water, and, although I cannot use water to demonstrate this for fear of flooding this beautiful auditorium"—he paused in response to the faint murmur of laughter—"I can demonstrate the Coanda Effect on air. In fact, this is something that even a child can do."

Richards took out a curved piece of paper from under the lectern and placed it on the table. He blew gently across the paper, at right-angles to the axis of the curve, and sure enough, the paper obediently rose.

"This is a principle used in flight aerodynamics," continued Richards, "with a stream of air bending itself around the convex curve of an aeroplane wing, to provide the aeroplane with lift. What is remarkable about the Coanda Effect is its strength, as it can pull a stream of water for a considerable distance around a curved object and, of course, contributes substantially to lifting heavy aeroplanes into the air."

The engineer again turned towards the stadium model on the table.

"In the case of our football stadium, we will look to shape the stadium roof in order to maximise the advantages of the Coanda Effect. The structure will be designed to actually accelerate the laminar flow of the passing air mass, concentrating the wind in the places where the turbines will be positioned.

"Further gains in energy yield can be achieved through the positioning of the turbines, and also through clever turbine design as demonstrated in research carried out in 2002 by my colleague Professor Stankovic."

Richards turned, extending his arm to introduce Professor Sinisa Stankovic, who was seated behind him and to his right. "Professor Stankovic proved that a structure located in a typical urban setting, with a built-in horizontal-axis wind turbine, can provide an annual energy yield that is 25 percent more than that of a large, free-standing propeller such as we are accustomed to seeing throughout the world."

"Yes, an increase of *at least* 25 percent," added Stankovic, a tanned, middle-aged Serb with grey, slightly unruly curly hair.

"Turbines having a free-standing position on a roof," continued Richards, gesturing towards the model of the football stadium in front of him, "will further improve performance, in comparison with turbines that are mounted in a duct within a building."

"But that doesn't make sense!" came a voice from the audience. "Surely, the optimum position for a wind turbine would be in the middle of the sea, or a flat plain, where the wind can pass through uninterrupted, with no friction to slow it."

All heads turned, searching for the source of scepticism.

Standing was a girl in her early twenties with a short, pixie-like hairstyle and rather masculine black-rimmed glasses. She was near the entrance to the auditorium. Richards resented interruptions from the audience, but on this occasion, he welcomed the intervention—having anticipated this very assertion.

"Thank you for broaching that," he said to the young woman. "The Coanda Effect does, certainly on its face, appear to be counterintuitive. But it is actually not the case. In any moving air mass, there will be natural turbulence and movement so that winds will blow past a given point in several directions. Even a turbine that is designed to move in order to face the prevailing wind direction will only be able to adapt to a certain extent. Far greater efficiency can be achieved by designing the curvature of urban structures so that they direct and channel airflows to enhance wind speeds where the turbines are located."

The young woman sank back in her seat.

David Carter, a member of the expert panel who had published extensively in the *Journal of Wind Engineering and Industrial Aerodynamics*, was anxious to make his mark on the discussion, and saw the interruption from the floor as an opportunity. He was keen to prevent Richards from disseminating the fruits of his life's work as his own.

"I should emphasise, at this point," Carter began, tapping the end of a sturdy silver pen on the panellists table, "that large, flat rooves such as those found on most modern sports stadia are ideal for this purpose, as they tend to be of low pitch and provide an extensive area of attached flow, with low correlations between the pressure fluctuations acting on different parts."

Richards stepped back half a pace, deferring to Carter. Encouraged, Carter, a stout man in his early sixties with a pockmarked and slightly reddened complexion, continued, explaining the behaviour of air masses when meeting a windward obstruction.

Carter stood and removed from his jacket pocket a telescopic, stainless-steel pointer that he frequently used during lectures. "In the case of this particular construction, as the air mass approaches a building of this nature, wind movement is initially normal. At the top of this windward wall"—he waved the steel stick from one end of the crest of the model stadium's wall to the other—"the airflow separates from the wall and then reattaches itself onto the roof. This forms a *separation bubble*. The length of this bubble depends upon the amount of turbulence in the wind flow; the more turbulence there is, the shorter the length of the separation bubble."

As Carter spoke, Richards relaxed now that he was temporarily no longer the focus of the audience's attention. He glanced around the room once again, his own attention passing from one face to the other. *An assassin?* he wondered with each face he scanned. *Could there possibly be somebody here capable of killing me?*

All night long, he had wrestled with how seriously he should take Merisi's warnings and his claims of coming from a future world. At the time, the stranger's story had seemed very convincing. Yet, as a scientist, it was natural for Richards to maintain a certain level of scepticism. Everything about Merisi's story was utterly fantastic.

On the other hand, it was not uncommon for Richards to succumb to paranoia, a result of the childhood trauma of losing his mother. Many of his close friends had advised him to seek counselling—all to no avail as his instinct had always been to shun medical assistance, and to self-manage. When Rossini had asked him about it in the car on the way to Milan, he explained it away as a tendency to daydream. But deep down he knew that it was a far more fundamental aspect of his psychology.

Now, surrounded by so many people that he did not know, the paranoia was winning the battle for control. Richards' attention returned to Carter's exposition when his fellow wind engineer mentioned his name.

"As I am sure Dr. Richards will concur, when a wind encounters a shallow obstacle, the initial effect will be for its speed to decrease slightly as it begins its journey up the slope," he continued, waving his hands to mimic airflow. "Gradually, the wind accelerates as it rises towards the crest of the obstruction, with maximum acceleration occurring at the crest, or slightly upwind of it. In terms of the vertical gradients within the air mass, the greatest speed-up effect is seen close to the surface of the object in question, with wind speed decreasing away from this surface—"

"That is why it is important that the turbines are not positioned too far from a roof's surface," interjected Richards.

"Exactly!" added Carter.

As Richards looked at Carter, he caught sight of Bryce-Fairbrother. In an instant, it occurred to him that the danger to his life—if there really was one—might not come from the audience but rather from behind him where the panellists sat. Suddenly, he remembered reading something about Bryce-Fairbrother in the newspapers, about him having pursued a military career. Richards was also aware that this *celebrity* economist had been orphaned at a very early age. *The classic profile of the MI5 recruit,* he thought. *Public school education and no emotional development as an infant. First perceptions can be deceived. Never judge a book by its cover; he's a grafter with a point to prove.* Perhaps Richards' dislike of Bryce-Fairbrother was fuelling his paranoia.

"It is important," continued Carter, raising his right index finger, "to site the turbines so that they are not within the separation bubble created at the crest of a stadium's roof, so the best locations are here—and here." He used his pointer to indicate a position near the outer edge of the roof, and then another, closer to the centre of the stadium.

"But you appear to be assuming that a turbine with a horizontal axis is the only option."

The latest intervention, in immaculate English, albeit with a trademark Dutch lisp, came from Dr. Sander Martens, who approached Carter. Dressed in designer jeans, a casual beige jacket and a pale-blue, open-necked shirt, Dr. Martens had founded and ran his own consultancy in Delft, in The Netherlands. Previously, he had completed a PhD on aerodynamics in the context of building-mounted wind turbines. In his late forties, Martens' fashionable facial stubble matched the closely shaven hair on the back and sides of his head.

Richards and Carter, slightly startled, turned to face the new arrival.

"An alternative would be something like this!" continued the Dutchman. As Martens passed Richards, he swiftly produced a metal object that flashed brightly as it caught the lights of the stage. To Richards it looked like a short knife. He flinched, jerking his head back sharply. Martens continued to the lectern, and Richards saw that the object was actually a scale model of a vertical turbine blade. It looked more like an egg whisk than a knife.

Richards glanced nervously at the row of panel members who were still seated and then scanned the audience. It appeared that nobody had noticed his initial reaction to Martens. Nevertheless, a layer of cold sweat developed between his shirt collar and his neck, and a bead of it ran down his back. He breathed slowly to regain his composure.

Martens continued. "This is a turbine design with a vertical axis. According to blade element momentum theory, a turbine like this should have a power advantage over the horizontal-axis designs in conditions of skewed flow. This is because it has a greater rotor area in contact with undisturbed flows." To illustrate his point, Martens held his whisk up against the stadium model, taking up a central position on the stage.

"I disagree," challenged Richards, who then repeated the case for the horizontal-axis wind turbine. Richards argued that a horizontal axis required less turbulence and would be positioned nearer to the centre of the roof. This viewpoint provoked yet another intervention from a panel member, and this time it was aggressive.

"No! No! No!" cried a voice with a trace of a Scottish accent. The speaker punctuated each word by slapping the flat of his hand on the table. "Do ye no' understand the basic principles of engineering?"

Neil McCrae, a structural engineer with a lifetime's experience in the building of stadia and warehouses and similar structures, was a rotund, moustachioed former rugby player. He bounded across the stage towards the experts gathered around the stadium model like witches at a cauldron. McCrae produced a sharp-looking penknife as his pointer, which rather put Martens' whisk-like turbine in the shade. Richards felt apprehensive as the knife-wielding Scot approached. He exhaled once McCrae had passed him. Emphatically tapping the inner rim of the stadium roof with the implement and addressing Richards, McCrae continued.

"What you are suggesting, laddie, is the positioning of a taller and heavier turbine in this position, which would need a substantial cantilever structure to support it."

"It needn't be heavy," countered Richards. He explained that a horizontal-axis turbine could have the required height to be above the turbulence that was close to the surface of the roof but still have a lightweight design using modern materials.

"But the beauty of my vertical-axis turbine," argued Martens now that it was clear that Richards' presentation had become a free-for-all argument, "is that it is tri-dimensional, and so can rotate 360 degrees, enabling it to align itself to catch the wind from whichever direction it is blowing."

"But, Sander," insisted Richards, "the whole point of my explanation of the Coanda Effect was to explain that the stadium will be built in such a way as to channel a *consistent* flow of air towards the roof-mounted turbines. And that, ladies and gentlemen," he concluded with an air of triumph, turning away from the huddle of experts to address his audience, "is why the Coanda Effect is so important to this design!"

Richards fell silent as a slight, slender woman made her way onto the stage. She strolled in slow and sultry fashion towards the throng of experts. The only sound in the auditorium was the regular and deliberate rhythm of her long stiletto heels on the hollow wooden stage. As she drew level with Richards, who was still standing next to the stadium model, she flicked out her right arm with another flash of metal and placed the back of her slim hand close to Richards' throat. The young engineer felt a sharp point pressing into the flesh just below his chin.

"It eez a nice toy you have here, Dottore," the woman whispered. She smiled, released him, and walked two paces towards the model on the table. Richards sighed with relief as he realised that the "instrument" was no more than the pointed fingernail of the woman's index finger, and the metallic flash had come from a chunky silver bracelet fitted tightly to her slender wrist.

"So! What do we know about your Coanda Effect, Dottore *Ree*-chards?" she went on, in a strong Italian accent. "It seems that it creates an accelerating effect within the predominant linear wind flow. This, in turn, enhances the wind yield obtained at the turbine positions through providing consistent and fast-flowing air."

The mysterious intruder moved towards Richards once again and straightened his tie. "You see, Dottore," she said, with a wink. "I am not just a pretty face! Relax, Dottore *Ree*-chards. A time will come for this venture."

Richards remained silent as he returned the gaze of those dark, slightly menacing eyes, not knowing what to make of this stranger, and having no idea what she meant by her words.

"I think," announced the conference chairman, who had been quite forgotten in the midst of all the drama, "that now would be a good time for a break."

CHAPTER 17

THE PATH FINDER

The hum of conversation in the conference hall echoed beneath the high vaulted ceiling as Dr. Ben Richards rejoined the main throng. He had taken advantage of the recess to freshen up and gather his thoughts. *Who on earth was that weird but remarkably attractive woman who interrupted before Giuffrè announced the coffee break? What does she want? And where is she now?* She had disappeared almost as stealthily as she arrived. *And where is Merisi?* There had been no sign of the man who declared himself to be Richards' protector.

Richards resolved to press on as planned. He had hoped to meet up with Grazia Rossini briefly before the seminar recommenced, but his diminutive companion was nowhere to be seen.

As he re-entered the large auditorium, Richards saw Volker Boer and Nadine Lester in earnest conversation with a gentleman sporting a neatly trimmed black beard and wearing a traditional Arab dishdasha. The sight of the long white robe meant only one thing to Richards—Arab money. *Just what we need,* he thought.

His gut instinct, a legacy of many years of chasing funding to develop his ideas, was to make a beeline for the new arrival and introduce himself, but he didn't want to appear presumptuous. "Don't be a fool, Ben," he said to himself. "Just because the man's an Arab, it doesn't mean that he's wealthy and that he has money to invest. He may well be a plumber!"

Ben smiled faintly to himself at the ridiculousness of his own thought. *Well, he's not carrying any tools,* he reasoned. But then something else occurred to him. *Could this Arabic gentleman possibly be a threat? Could he be the one with a vested commercial interest in eliminating me?* After all, such an apparently rich and powerful person could easily afford to hire someone to kill him. Richards glanced nervously around the room in a futile attempt to identify someone who looked like an assassin.

He resolved to make himself known to the Boer, Lester and the Arab, but the conference chairman beckoned to him frantically, reminding him that he was to introduce the final session of the day. Richards dutifully made his way to the stage.

As Richards approached the lectern, a dark-skinned, white-haired old man suddenly emerged from one of the small groups of people who had been milling around on the stage and stood directly in front of him. The old man stared straight into Ben's eyes with an intensity and gravity that stopped Ben in his tracks.

"*Chiaroscuro. Chiaroscuro,*" said the old man, in a hoarse voice that was barely audible above the murmur of the delegates sprinkled around the hall. "Shades of darkness will come to your foreground if you do not look out for the lighter shades in your background."

The words meant nothing to Richards, and, for a second time that afternoon, he was rendered speechless. The old man appeared to be harmless enough, but such was Richards' heightened state of alert following Merisi's warnings that he was suspicious of the man's motives. He was about to demand an explanation but was interrupted by the raised voice of the conference chairman.

"Ladies and gentlemen. Please return to your seats, as the next session is about to begin."

Richards turned to see Giuffrè with microphone in hand, still beckoning to him.

He felt a warm but wrinkled hand clutch him by the wrist. His attention returned to the old man, who continued to stare at him intently. "Take this," said the stranger, pressing a folded card into Richards' hand.

"Are you ready to introduce the next session, Dottore?" asked the conference chairman.

The stranger took the hint that it was time for him to vacate the stage. But before leaving, he said, "Let me pour you a fresh glass of water, Dr. Richards. With all of that talking and debate you surely must be parched."

The old man walked briskly to the lectern and filled a glass for Richards from the crystal jug that had been placed on the small table nearby. He removed the half-full glass Richards had been using before the recess.

"It's time to start," the chairman chimed. "I will call the meeting to order, Dottore,"

"Of course," replied Richards. He glanced over his shoulder to see the old man trot down the small flight of stairs at the end of the stage and disappear among the many delegates criss-crossing as they returned to their seats.

"The focus of this final session," began the chairman, "is about the detail of the engineering challenges associated with harnessing wind flow activity in the most optimal way, and I would like to give the floor, once again, to Dr. Ben Richards."

Richards swiftly stashed the card that the old man had given him in his trouser pocket and struggled to focus on the task at hand, especially as he could see the unmistakable figure of the Arab gentleman seated in the middle of the back row. And there was still no sign of Merisi—or Grazia Rossini.

The session was held in a goldfish-bowl format intended to encourage more interaction with the audience. During the interval, the seating on the stage had been arranged so that the experts were in a semi-circle around a coffee table, with the lectern that Richards was now using positioned just to their left. It occurred to Richards that he would rather not have his back to any section of the audience. For now, however, he was happy to be facing the mass of faces.

Recovering his composure, Richards provided a brief recap of the previous session's discussion, explaining that all present were welcome to ask questions and input their views after a short introduction provided by Nadine Lester.

"Nadine. Please—"

The shape-shifting android—a perfect copy of the University of Glasgow lecturer in every respect, and with a comprehensive database of her work downloaded into its memory—stood and approached the lectern. Richards smiled amiably at his colleague as she passed him and was slightly surprised that she did not seem to recognise him.

Lester's imposter took the microphone and without hesitation launched into a comprehensive explanation of the importance of the attachment of wind flow to the flat roof of a building, in order to maximise the consistency of the wind yield in such a location. She went into detail about the optimum location of roof-mounted wind turbines.

"Maximum yield can be achieved with two rows of turbines," she explained, "one row along the outer edge of the roof, and the other inside this, nearer to the centre of the roof."

"But, obviously, as this is a football ground," interrupted Richards, "we would need to be mindful of any impact caused by shadows being cast on the pitch, and there might be some roof strengthening required to take the weight of the turbines."

Lester turned her head to observe Richards as he spoke but said nothing, and her face betrayed no emotion.

"Any such retrofitting would not be required with a new stadium, which would have turbines included in its design, from the outset," continued Richards, rattled by Lester's blank stare.

Lester continued. "The best position for roof-mounted turbines would be farther away from the outer edge of the stadium, around about here," she explained, pointing to the preferred position on the football stadium model using the end of a long penknife.

"But what about the impact of ice and snow on the roof, in winter, and the effect of high winds whipping around the turbines?"

The voice came from the audience. Richards glanced around the room to see if he could recognise the questioner. But the android came straight back with an answer. Without looking up from the model, it retorted, "One of these turbines weighs 1.509 tonnes. A 30 cm covering of snow, spread over the 434.95 square metres of roof between roof supports, would increase this mass at the weakest point of the roof by 0.985 percent, which would not threaten the structural integrity of the roof."

Richards was shocked by the curtness and speed of the response, and the questioner was not going to contest such a precise and confident reply. Still using the knife as a pointer, Lester continued with barely a pause. "The other turbines should be positioned here, here, here, here and here," she concluded before returning to her seat.

"Thank you, Nadine," said Richards, standing. "The next expert that I would like to invite to make a brief presentation is Mr. Volker Boer, who is a wind engineer. One of the high-profile projects that Volker has worked on is the iconic Burj Khalifa building in Dubai." Richards paused, partly to let the impact of Boer's Burj Khalifa connection sink in with the audience, but also to give himself a second to find the brief biography on Boer that he had prepared in his conference notes.

Richards inhaled as he prepared to read the paragraph, but to his astonishment Boer was already at the lectern launching into his presentation.

"Thank you, Dr. Benjamin Richards," began the android. "To achieve the maximum wind yield from a roof-mounted turbine, there are certain advantages of a horizontal-axis wind turbine over a vertical-axis wind turbine." The Boer imposter then listed the reasons for using HAWTs.

As he did so, Richards slowly sank back into his seat, slightly miffed that he had not had the opportunity to introduce his colleague of some ten years, but also rather caught off guard by Boer's abrupt start. *Dr. Benjamin Richards? He usually calls me Ben,* Richards thought.

Boer's demeanour seemed odd. Richards' attention drifted away from his friend's presentation, and he began to muse over the many strange occurrences of that day.

I feel a bit like Alice in Wonderland, he thought. *Yet this is by no means a pleasant dream.*

Boer continued, showing detailed maps and diagrams using an overhead projector, but without having to refer to notes. He described the winds that affected the British Isles, which was where Richards was intending to implement his ideas for urban wind-power generation. Boer argued that because Britain's weather was dominated by south-westerlies, it was not necessary for a turbine to have a complex axis that could point its blades in any direction.

"So, with such a consistent prevailing wind flow," he argued, "there is no reason not to use the tried and tested horizontal-axis technology, positioning the turbines perpendicular to the predominant windward flow coming from the southwest of the British Isles." He then stopped as abruptly as he had begun and returned to his seat.

The contrast between the beam of the overhead projector and the ambient darkness that surrounded it had caused Richards' mind to wander once again. This time, his thoughts returned to what the old man had said to him about shades of darkness coming to his foreground. *Lighter shades in my background? And what was all that about chiaroscuro? What was the old fella trying to tell me?*

Richards became aware of the sudden silence. Eyes were turned expectantly towards him. He distractedly looked at the time, drifting into a trance as he imagined he heard the ticking of his watch. A tremor of disturbed thought crossed his mind. *What time will there be an attempt on my life?* Then, just like that, he snapped out of it and returned to the lectern.

"Many thanks, Volker; or should I say, many thanks, Professor Volker Jacobus Boer?" he said, smiling playfully at his friend. Boer made no response, maintaining a fixed gaze into the audience.

Richards continued. "I would like to thank both of my colleagues for their contribution to this discussion. To sum up, regardless of the detail of the type of turbine we use and the position of the turbines on the roof, the most important question for the whole idea of urban wind generation concerns whether the owner of a large building with a flat roof, such as a football stadium, can be persuaded to pilot the technology. In short, a persuasive business case needs to be made to encourage an enterprising entrepreneur to come forward."

"Which is where *I* come in," said a clear and confident voice from over Richards' right shoulder. He immediately recognised it as belonging to Richard Bryce-Fairbrother. Richards turned to look at Bryce-Fairbrother, as much to draw the audience's attention to the new speaker as to confirm the young man's identity. Then, speaking through the microphone again and making a conscious effort to avoid any hint of irony or sarcasm, he said, "We are indeed very fortunate to have with us an economist who knows all about investment in this field. Mr.—"

"Bryce-Fairbrother. Professor Richard Bryce-Fairbrother, actually, although I left academia behind many moons ago," he added with a slight chuckle.

"And what can you tell us, Professor?" asked Richards politely.

"Well, the issue you are going to have with this idea is the start-up costs. It's all very well for the tree huggers and the beard-and-sandals brigade to dream of clean and sustainable energy, but somebody needs to outlay considerable investment. In my experience, that will be hard to come by for such an unproven technology."

For a moment or two, there was a heavy silence as the audience contemplated the ruthlessness with which Bryce-Fairbrother had dismissed Richards' ideas. Richards steeled himself against the beard-and-sandals jibe, which always irritated him.

"Well," continued Richards, "I am convinced that this is an economically viable technology, and that football stadiums will have the most potential, given that they tend to be situated in major cities, and that they are used for relatively few hours per week, which leaves plenty of scope for selling electricity back to the national grid.

"The first objective is to set up an initial pilot scheme. If I can persuade one major football club with a suitable stadium to host that pilot and demonstrate the clear benefits of urban wind-power generation, then I am convinced that others will follow. Once this idea gathers momentum, then similar schemes can be rolled out in other cities, and soon the whole world will see that this is the way forward in the twenty-first century.

"I have here a sketch that I have drawn of what a stadium with roof-mounted wind turbines might look like." He placed a transparent slide onto the glass of the projector. "As you can see, the turbines are positioned in such a way as to—" Suddenly, Richards felt a faint disturbance of air just below his left ear, and his presentation was cut short by a loud crack as the light of the projector was extinguished.

There was confusion as the auditorium was plunged into near darkness. Then a murmur rose from the audience—swiftly overtaken by the wail of a fire alarm. A few members of the audience cried out. As people's eyes became accustomed to the gloom, the shapes of conference centre staff could be seen hurrying onto the stage, escorting the panel of experts away. The fluorescent security lights suspended from the high ceiling flickered on and then shone brightly, and Richards now saw that other members of staff had begun to evacuate the audience.

He alone of all those present knew that that bulb had not simply blown. Somebody had fired a projectile of some kind, and maybe this was the shot that was intended to take his life. *Who fired that shot?* he wondered. *And where did it come from?* He quivered with fright. *Merisi was right, it seems,* he thought.

With the lighting in the auditorium restored, he was able to glance around the rapidly emptying seats that faced the stage. There was nothing suspicious to be seen among the cosmopolitan collection of businessmen, consultants and academics. But one unmistakable absentee was the traditionally dressed Arab whose striking white dishdasha had previously marked him out from the crowd. *And where is Bryce-Fairbrother?* He was nowhere to be seen.

Richards had little time to dwell on whether the Arab gentleman's absence might be significant as a young, female conference attendant took him by the arm, ushering him to an exit door at the back of the stage.

"This way, please," she said.

"Yes, of course," replied Richards. But as he turned to follow her, he became aware of a strange, pale-blue light at the end of the back row of seats in the auditorium. He jerked his head around to see what it was, but there was nothing to be seen.

"Did you see that?" he asked the girl.

"See what?" she answered.

Richards paused, as he was not entirely sure what he had seen himself.

"I'm sorry, but we really must leave the stage as quickly as possible," the girl insisted.

As they passed the projector, Richards noticed among a thousand tiny shards of glass on the floor a small, feathered dart that looked remarkably like the one he had picked up at the Ponte Vecchio. He veered away and bent to pick it up quickly and surreptitiously. As he rose, popping the projectile into the inside pocket of his jacket, he once again felt the warmth of a woman's hand on his arm. But this time it was the tanned and manicured hand of the brown-eyed Italian beauty who had approached him at the end of the opening session of the seminar.

"It eez quite a day that you are having, Dottore Ree-chards," she said. "Meet me at Caravaggio's restaurant at eight this evening." Then she melted away into the crowd evacuating the auditorium in an orderly fashion, leaving Richards standing on the stage, wondering what to make of what had indeed been quite a day.

• •

Lester felt the softness of the cotton duvet against her cheek as she awoke. Just inches away was Volker's familiar soft breathing—yet something was not quite right.

As she recovered consciousness, Lester realised that all was dark apart from a thin, vertical sliver of light in front of her. Suddenly, she sensed that she was in a very confined space, and when it became clear that she could barely move her arms and legs, she screamed—the legacy of many past nightmares of being buried alive.

"Arrgh! Volker! Volker!"

Boer woke up with a start and instinctively thrust his arms forward. The involuntary spasm was enough to force the doors of the wardrobe open, and the couple covered their eyes as the hotel room was suddenly drowned in bright afternoon sunshine. Boer was the first to regain his senses and lifted Lester out of the wardrobe and onto a chair. As his eyes adjusted to the light, he caught sight of the red, illuminated display of the room's clock-radio.

"It's bloody four o'clock in the afternoon!" he exclaimed. "What the hell was in those cocktails last night?"

CHAPTER 18

THE THREE
CONSPIRATORS

As the confused crowd of delegates loitered in front of the Instituto di Energia, the old man with the white hair slipped away from the chatter and the gathering pall of cigarette smoke, striding down the grey stone steps that led to the busy main road outside. With a nimbleness that belied his wrinkled, elderly appearance, the man dodged between the two lines of traffic crawling slowly in either direction. He arrived at a small, grassless park consisting of a stone-and-bronze war memorial with four wrought iron benches facing it at each point of the compass. He sat in the shade of a young lime tree, which hid him from view of the people gathered in front of the institute.

He took out a disc-like device from the pocket of his tweed jacket and slid an index finger across its surface. Almost as soon as his tanned face had been illuminated by a blue light, a woman spoke with great urgency: "Merisi!"

"Yes," replied the old man. Then, without hesitating, he began his report to UNA.

"It is done. The assassination of Ben Richards has been averted, but I fear that my work here is not yet complete. Somebody tried to drug the target's drink during one of the seminar intervals. I managed to intervene before he drank it, although it leaves me in no doubt that Shui Feng was in the room."

"Did you see him?"

"No, of course not. I took a close look at everyone in the auditorium, but Feng could have taken on the identity of any one of the delegates."

"Did he see you?"

"No, I am undercover myself. I have adopted the appearance of an old man today. It is a disguise that Feng is yet to see."

"Where is Richards now?"

"I'm not sure. The whole building has been evacuated. The delegates on the stage were led out through the back door of the building, so he must be in that group. I am about to go and find him."

"Yes, that's extremely important, Merisi. You must locate him, and then not let him out of your sight. But before you go, I have some important intelligence to pass on to you." Merisi had taken a few steps towards the open gate of the small park but stopped and listened.

"Go on," he said.

"We have received information from a reliable source inside GIATCOM," continued the woman. "Far from wanting Richards dead, Shui Feng has orders to bring him back here to the present. We do not know their full purpose, but they must NOT be allowed to succeed in this."

"I knew that cunning little prick would be up to something like that. That explains the slight shimmer of Richards' water just before I replaced it. Feng must have put tarminium, or maybe septinitro, in his glass to put him to sleep, although both would have been very slow to act."

"But there is no time to wonder about that," insisted the woman. "Just locate Richards as soon as you can. And I think you need to make him aware of exactly who, and what, is pursuing him."

"Of course. Understood."

Merisi left the cover of the park, extinguishing his device as he went, and the old man skipped across the road through the increasingly busy traffic.

. .

Richards found himself alone, albeit in a crowd of people milling around a long, narrow courtyard at the back of the Instituto di Energia. This was the area set aside for the institute's fire drills and evacuations, which was where the conference delegates were being corralled while security staff checked the building for hazards.

The tarmacked area was bathed in afternoon sunshine, with the brick wall of the institute on one side and a cream-coloured, plaster wall on the other, both reflecting a pleasant warmth onto the slightly bewildered but mostly relaxed gathering of delegates. The courtyard was filled with all the paraphernalia and detritus of modern living—dustbins, bicycles, Vespa scooters and cage trolleys carelessly left in the general vicinity of the institute. Beyond the perimeter wall, which stood some fifteen feet high, Richards could see the uppermost floors of apartment buildings with metal shutters on the windows and washing being aired on the railings of every balcony.

At one end of the courtyard was a service road, but at the other was the Via Orbassano, a street with many cafés, bars and restaurants, and a favourite after-work destination for the academics and white-collar employees nearby.

Richards attempted to call Rossini but found that the signal to his mobile phone was unable to penetrate the urban canyon surrounding him.

I wonder what they're doing in there, he thought. *There's certainly no point in looking for whoever it was who fired that thing at me.*

Richards realised that the only evidence of any consequence was nestled in his pocket. He took out the dart to examine it, turning towards the courtyard wall so that the object was hidden from his fellow loiterers. There could be no doubt about the similarity between the two projectiles that had recently been aimed in his direction. He no longer harboured any doubt that everything Merisi had told him was true. The one mystery remaining was why he was still alive. *Why did the dart miss its mark? Could Merisi have had a hand in this?*

Richards decided that it would be unwise to provide any evidence that either incident had taken place. So he wrapped the dart in his handkerchief and put it back in his pocket. No members of the institute's staff were in view, and with the closing time for the conference now passed, the many small clusters of people who had been happily chatting away in Italian drifted off into the bars and restaurants in the Via Orbassano.

Richards would do the same just as soon as he was able to enter the building to retrieve his documents folder and stationery. All he wanted—apart from a cold beer—was to meet up with Grazia Rossini again and try to make some sense of the day's events. He checked his phone for text messages for the fourth time since stepping out from the auditorium. *Nothing!*

With no information from the institute staff about whether it was safe to re-enter the building, Richards decided to creep back into the auditorium to see what was going on. As he approached the rear entrance to the building, he saw at the end of the fast-emptying courtyard the unmistakable figure of the raven-haired Italian woman he had arranged to meet later that evening.

At first, Richards was content to fix his gaze on her long, slim legs as she sauntered across the courtyard. But he was surprised to observe the woman stop and converse with a man and a woman who he immediately recognised as Volker Boer and Nadine Lester. The three obviously knew one another and were standing close together, conversing quietly and indemonstrably. Absent was the smiling and gesticulation one might expect with more casual acquaintances, or even with people meeting for the first time.

I wonder what that's all about, thought Richards. *How does this woman know Volker and Nadine? In fact, who the hell is she?*

Richards was interrupted by the vibration of the mobile phone in his pocket. Hurriedly, he activated the screen. His initial feeling was one of disappointment that it was not Grazia trying to get in touch with him, but then his face froze with amazement. It was Volker Boer.

Sorry to miss your presentation, Ben, the message read. *Nadine and I have gone down with a particularly nasty bout of food poisoning.*

Richards looked across the narrow courtyard at his two friends still standing in the street and gave his phone one more puzzled look.

• •

"So, nothing has changed," said Feng to the Boer and Lester doppelgangers. As planned, Feng had morphed into the form of an attractive local woman. "You will meet with Sheikh Bader bin Almahdi at Caravaggio's restaurant at seven thirty. Have you both downloaded all the technical information that you need?"

"Yes," said the two androids.

Changing his appearance was very much part of Feng's armoury. As a product of the military wing of GIATCOM's Enhanced Human Programme, Feng lacked the ability to alter his own molecular structure, which was the shape-shifting technique employed by the TX-series androids. However, his skill with prosthetics, with the assistance of other twenty-second-century technologies, enabled him to alter the tone and pitch of his voice. He could temporarily adjust his oestrogen levels, which meant that he was capable of convincingly adopting the persona of a woman without the disadvantages of the robotic and mechanical gestures that betrayed the disguise of the TX-series.

In 2112, the performance of TX1 and TX2 would have immediately been recognised as a thinly veiled attempt at impersonation. Miles Cardus and GIATCOM had staked everything on the belief that, in an era when even the most sophisticated robots were nothing more than mechanical components of a production line, shape-shifting TX-series androids would be able to assume the identity of a human without too many questions being asked.

"Remember," continued Feng, "Sheikh Bader is a Muslim, and so he will not be taking alcohol, but you may do so, provided that you limit yourselves to one glass of wine each. That's important, as your digestive systems are not designed to absorb alcohol. The sheikh will pay for the meal. Have you downloaded information on what you should order?"

"Yes," they replied again in unison.

"Now, the sheikh will arrive with an entourage of people, who will all be armed, but this is normal. So they are not to be neutralised. Understand?"

"Yes."

"When you first meet the sheikh, you are to address him as Your Excellency. After that, you call him sir. In terms of the negotiations, allow the sheikh to state his case and explain his intentions. Merely answer his technical questions using the information that you have downloaded. Do not try to lead the conversation, as this will appear to the sheikh as being impertinent—especially you, TX2, as you have the persona of a female human, and as such he will expect you to speak only when spoken to. Is that understood?"

"Yes," replied TX2.

"The sheikh will offer to provide you with a large amount of money to fund your ongoing research. This you will accept gratefully and thank His Excellency for his outstanding generosity. Remember, whatever happened back in the auditorium, this meeting with the sheikh has already taken place in history. So, your immediate objective is to make sure that you do exactly what Lester and Boer did originally. We can deal with the detail of the sheikh's future plans later."

Feng looked earnestly into the lifeless eyes of the two androids, raising his carefully manicured index fingers in a gesture that emphasised the importance of what he was about to say next.

"What you *must* understand is that the failed attempt to assassinate Richards means that, from now on, a new course of history is being created. Everything that he now does, and everything that happens to people around him, constitute new events, whose impact on the future can only be guessed at. If he should cause a female to conceive, then this might create generations of previously unborn humans. Much worse, if he were to cause an incident that results in the death of a young human, then that might wipe out generations that had previously lived."

Feng could detect no semblance of understanding in the expression of either of the TX androids. "Do you understand what I am saying to you?" he hissed.

"Yes," they replied.

"Well, just ensure that you make no mistakes with the Arab. Do you have any questions?"

"Yes," said TX1.

There was a pause of several seconds as Feng waited for the android's question. The TX series had limitations when it came to the subtleties of human interaction.

"Come on, then. What is your question?" Feng demanded with growing impatience.

"What happened in the auditorium?" asked TX1. "Did things go according to your plan?"

"Yes, things went precisely according to the plan," exclaimed Feng. "I managed to administer the drug to Richards' water during the interval, and it will take effect in about four hours."

Feng paused before continuing. "However, Merisi is here, and we know that the UNA has been sent here to stop Richards' assassination. What Merisi doesn't know, of course, is that I am here to drug Richards—not kill him. It hasn't entered his limited mind that Richards might be worth more to us alive than dead."

The two androids stared blankly at Feng.

"I am sure," he continued, "that Merisi was responsible for blocking my attempt to sedate Richards in Florence, and then I thought I caught a glimpse of him in Siena. I have been keeping an eye out for him ever since. We can take Richards this evening. I have invited him to have dinner with me at Caravaggio's, the same restaurant where you are meeting with Almahdi. So, watch out for him."

"How do you know he will come?" asked the female android.

"He'll be there. According to our research, my current appearance means that I am irresistible for a single male of his age and phenotype. I have gone to a great deal of effort, as you can both see."

Feng paused with a self-congratulatory smile, but there was no reaction from his team members. Feng sighed. "Not that you two would appreciate that. That's what I hate about working with droids."

The two stared ahead unfazed, awaiting Feng's instruction.

"Anyway, I'm afraid that Dr. Richards will be disappointed, as I will not be turning up for the date. I will leave it to you two to keep an eye on him and to record anything that he says onto your memory. I will be close by.

"And there is something else, which might play to our advantage," added Feng, as much to himself as to his designated co-conspirators. "Richards arrived at the seminar with a companion. A young female. I didn't know about her, but she may prove useful to us. I don't know what her relationship is to Richards, but keep an eye out for her this evening."

The androids nodded, although neither had the capacity to consider what they might do if they were to see Grazia Rossini, and neither were equipped to understand the significance of any relationship she might have with Richards. Feng, on the other hand, was already formulating plans for using Rossini to manipulate Richards.

For all his enhanced physical and sensory powers, Feng's most potent weapon was his ability to understand the psychology of his opponents, and the instinct he had developed for recognising and exploiting people's weaknesses. This was the part of Feng's armoury that Merisi had come to respect and fear above all others, and this was the reason why Merisi closely shadowed Richards. Preventing Feng from engaging directly with Richards was Merisi's top priority.

"Did you have any problems with Lester and Boer at the hotel?" asked Feng.

"No," said TX1.

"I hope that you did not cause any tissue damage, or leave any signs of a struggle in the room?"

"No," replied TX2. "We tidied them up and put them away so that we left the room as we had found it."

"What do you mean you tidied them up and put them away?"

"We packed them neatly in the room out of sight, according to training module 5(11.9)."

Feng began to wonder what had taken place when the GIATCOM androids carried out the identity acquisition procedure on Boer and Lester. But he realised that there was now no means of going back to correct any errors.

"But are you sure that you left them undamaged?"

"Yes," they said.

"Well, there's nothing that we can do about any mess you've made now. I need to get you both to Caravaggio's and get you seated at the table that the sheikh has reserved. And remember that Lester and Boer are a couple, and remember also that Lester is a female, TX2, so you need to behave in a feminine manner, just like me. And remember that your most important objective, which is to—"

Feng stopped and looked behind him, gazing on a large, industrial refuse bin in the alleyway just off the main pedestrian thoroughfare. He raised an index finger in the direction of TX1 and TX2, commanding them to be still and remain silent. As he crept towards the bin, he removed a small hand-held device that he had concealed in the small leather bag that matched his close-fitting Gucci dress. Feng stopped. He remained motionless, still listening, with his hypersensitive eyes fixed upon the bin. Then, with a sudden movement, he raised the device and activated it.

There was a flash of white light, barely visible to the passers-by in the late-afternoon sunshine. Next a muffled sizzling noise emanated from behind the bin. Feng sprang forward to examine the remains of the biological lifeform that his senses had detected. Behind the bin, a wisp of grey smoke lingered next to the wall. A patch of black residue on the tarmac was all that remained of what had previously been a cat, or maybe a small dog, foraging among the refuse.

Feng returned to the androids, who had obediently remained in position.

"It was nothing," reported Feng. "A small creature of some kind."

He looked around, observing the people hurrying from their offices in pairs and groups of three and four. He paid special attention to anyone that walked alone, mindful that Merisi, his nemesis, was a master of disguise.

"We have to go, now," he said. "Follow me."

The trio joined the rest of the Milanese in what was now a busy Via Orbassano.

CHAPTER 19

ITALIAN CONNECTIONS

Richards' drive from the auditorium to the apartment mostly consisted of crawling through Milan's congested streets amidst a cacophony of car horns and impatiently revved engines. Yet the chaos in the streets provided some solitude after the hectic and incident-packed afternoon.

Foremost in his mind was the mystery of the red dart, and the whereabouts of Rossini—plus, the gorgeous Italian woman who had brazenly invited him to dinner that evening.

"Oooh!" Ben said out loud. "What do I do about her?"

With so many confused thoughts swirling around in his head, he had quite forgotten about those brown eyes—and those legs! It had also not occurred to him that he might have a dilemma to solve concerning his plans for the evening. Thoughts of getting back together with Rossini after the conference had been uppermost in his mind all day, but it was not every day that such an attractive woman came up to him and asked him out to dinner.

What is she after? What are her motives? he wondered.

Perhaps she represented a route to funding, perhaps as a backer for his business plans. Eventually, a combination of curiosity and greed got the better of Richards, and he decided that he simply had to attend his dinner date at eight. *But what will I tell Grazia? How will she react to me seeing another woman?*

Richards used the rest of the drive to consider a plan and had one by the time he swung the car off the Via Giambellino and manoeuvred the rented Lancia Kappa down into the underground car park of the plush apartment complex. He wearily hauled himself up the stairs at the rear of the property and opened the door with the key that Rossini had given him.

"Grazia," he called out. But there was no response.

Richards dumped his keys and documents folder on an expensively upholstered armchair in the corner of the room and dialled Rossini's mobile number using the hotel's landline.

Richards thought he might have misdialled and tried again. This time there was no mistake, and no doubt about who it was with the soft-spoken Italian accent that answered his call.

"*Pronto?*"

"Grazia, it's Ben."

"Oh, Ben! Where have you been? I thought you were going to call me during the first coffee break."

"Yes, I tried but I couldn't get a signal anywhere. I've just got back to the apartment. Where are you?"

"I've had to pop into our Milan office, I'm afraid," answered Grazia, "and I'm going to be here until quite late . . . So, how did it go?"

"Not bad—except for someone trying to kill me, and friends I thought were close friends acting like they barely know me."

"What?"

Richards related the incident about the dart and the strange behaviour of Lester and Boer.

"Are you sure the dart was aimed at you?" she asked.

"Well, I felt it brush against my cheek, so I'm pretty convinced. Although the fact that the dart missed me might be significant. Maybe whoever fired it missed me deliberately; it was a warning."

"Well, it sounds like a very similar incident to the one at the Ponte Vecchio that you were telling me about."

"And the dart was very similar to the one I found on the ground on that day. I'll show it to you later."

"You mean you have the dart?" Rossini asked.

"Yes, it's here in my hand."

"Well, why didn't you hand it in to the police? I assume that you have reported the incident?"

"Well, not exactly."

"Why not? This is a very serious matter."

"I was going to, but—"

"I can't believe that the institute's security people weren't all over the scene. I assume that the head of security called the police in?"

"Oh, the police came and the auditorium was evacuated, but when I went back into the building to collect my things, there were just a few junior police officers manning the scene, and of course none spoke English."

"Well, I'm very worried about you. I'm on my way over, right now. My article can wait."

"Well, don't come over just yet. You see, I need to meet someone for dinner at eight." Ben winced, and there was a pause.

"Dinner? Who with? And where?" Rossini asked with a hint of jealousy.

"It's at a restaurant called Caravaggio's, and with some German bloke I met at the conference." Ben winced again.

"What German bloke? What is his name?" Rossini pressed.

It suddenly occurred to Ben that the mysterious brunette had not given him a name, so he could honestly say that he didn't know, but he felt that he had better think of a German name—a man's name.

"Herman . . . somebody," he said with minimal hesitation. "He didn't give me his surname. He's someone high up in the German Ministry of Energy. He seems very interested in my work. He might be an important contact."

"Herman the German!" exclaimed Grazia with a hint of scepticism. "And why can't I join you? Is it a case of no dogs, no Italians or something?"

"No, nothing like that. It's just that it'll be two boring men talking about work. That's all."

There was another short silence.

"Anyway, why would a restaurant want to ban dogs?" asked Ben, trying to lighten the mood.

"That's not funny," Rossini said.

"I promise I won't be longer than I need to be—and if all goes well, I'll bring back a bottle of champagne."

"Better make it two bottles, then, and not cheap champagne."

"Of course not," replied Richards, relieved. "Right then," he said out loud after he had replaced the receiver on the wall beside the bed. "Let's see what Herman has to say for herself."

• •

Caravaggio's was situated in a side street just off the magnificent Piazzale Cardusio with its imposing, neoclassical buildings. Richards decided to take the metro into town, and as he emerged from Cordusio station on the escalator, he found the square bathed in warmth as the sun dipped into the horizon. He glanced at his watch, noting he was just a ten-minute walk from the restaurant.

Caravaggio's was an unexceptional establishment, with a small terrace encroaching onto the street. All of the tables on the terrace were already taken, and as he made his way to the open double doors at the entrance, Richards, a lifelong nonsmoker, marvelled at the enthusiasm with which the locals blended their cigarette smoke with the fumes of the passing traffic.

He wore a navy-blue shirt, white cotton trousers, and a light, burgundy sweater loosely tied around his neck. As he entered, he was surprised to find a calm and relaxed atmosphere within. Some of the tables were occupied by small family groups. Others hosted businessmen sitting alone, reading a newspaper and sipping espresso, unwinding from a day's work. At the far end of the restaurant, a young man with black, wavy hair was playing soft jazz on a piano.

It was eight and Richards scanned the room, but there was no sign of his date. So he ordered a drink from the bar.

"Martini, extra dry," he said. The bartender nodded and immediately reached for a glass.

Richards found a vacant table just a few feet away from the bar. In the ashtray he found a small spinning top that had no doubt been left there by a child. He sat idly spinning the translucent toy on the table, marvelling at the kaleidoscope of colours that emanated from it, making seemingly random patterns on the dark mahogany table. He was observing the thin strobes of light that penetrated the darkness around him when he was suddenly woken from his reverie.

"Impressive! Do you mind if I join you, Dottore?" It was Rossini wearing a red blouse speckled with the lights from Richards' toy.

"Huh? Grazia? What the devil are you doing here?"

"Better the devil you know instead of the devil you don't," she said. "I decided that you need looking after. We can't have you being accosted by a strange woman in a strange city like this, can we?" She gave Richards' hand a reassuring squeeze. Richards sat stunned and speechless but delighted to see the beautiful young journalist and flattered by her interest in *protecting* him.

"I figured that *Herman* may well be a *Hermine*, and that *she* might be devious. One has to be careful who one meets in dark places."

Richards stared into Rossini's eyes and knew he had been foiled by a good detective.

"I see," he mumbled. "Safety in numbers. Well, now that you're here, you must have a drink."

He sipped nervously at his martini, glancing to the bartender to place another order. But he suddenly had the feeling that something was not quite right. There was a stillness at each table. As the pianist continued, the music reached a crescendo, which seemed to sum up the moment. It appeared to Richards as if the occupants of each table were waiting to see who would make the first move. Was it just his paranoia?

On the other side of the restaurant he spotted Nadine Lester and Volker Boer speaking to the Arab gentleman that he had seen them with at the seminar. Richards was about to explain to Rossini that he had found their behaviour rather bizarre when he spotted, at a table much closer to him, the old man who had passed him that mysterious card during the seminar.

"Now, that is just weird," said Richards as he drained his martini glass and pulled a small wad of neatly folded cash from his trouser pocket. "Grazia, would you get me another martini, and whatever you want for yourself?"

"Of course."

"I just need to speak to someone. I'll be back in a minute."

Richards approached the old man with a feigned air of nonchalance, glancing over at the Arab gentleman and scanning the room for anything else that didn't quite seem right. The old man smiled amiably enough, as if he had been expecting Richards to come over and speak with him.

"Hello there," began Richards. "You disappeared, earlier, before I had the chance to—"

"Did you look carefully at the card?" the old man interrupted.

"Yes, I had a look at it," Richards lied. He removed the card from among his collection of credit cards and the business cards he had collected at the seminar.

"Sit down, Dottore," said the old man, gesturing at the empty seat in front of him. "Have a drink with me." He poured red wine into an empty water glass on the table for Richards. "Tell me what you think of this; it's a local Lombardy wine, produced by a small vineyard on the north shore of Lake Garda. There is something different about it, and I cannot put my finger on what it is."

Richards held the glass up to the light and imbibed a generous draught of the dark red.

"What do you think, Dottore? It is different, no?"

"Yes, I suppose it is," replied Richards, leery as to why the old gentleman wanted his opinion on a wine. "I am not a connoisseur of wine by any means, but I can see why this one is of interest to you. Yes, it's unusual."

The old man merely smiled at him.

"Yes, so this card you gave me—"

"Ah yes, the card."

Richards held the card in the light of the candle illuminating the crimson tablecloth, and both men cast their eyes onto the hand-written letters very deliberately arranged in two set patterns.

"This is a sator square, isn't it?" began Richards. "I know that it is an ancient symbol dating back to the days of the Holy Roman Empire."

The old man nodded.

"But what has it got to do with me?" asked Richards.

"Do not dismiss the knowledge of the Romans just because their scientists and engineers lived in a world that existed many centuries ago. They had not yet begun to destroy the environment. Nevertheless, their greatest thinkers applied themselves to the same problems that preoccupy your mind today. They strived hard to develop means of generating power for their industry, and they wished to do so as efficiently as possible. I understand that harnessing the power of the wind is your particular area of interest, Dottore?"

"Yes, of course. Well, you were at the seminar this afternoon."

"Yes, Dottore, and your ideas for urban power generation are very interesting, but hardly unprecedented."

There was a glint in the old man's eyes as he awaited Richards' response.

"So, what are you telling me? That the Romans had already developed their own wind turbines, and that they built them on top of the Colosseum?" he asked with a dismissive chuckle. The old man said nothing as his expression remained stoic. "So, you *are* trying to tell me this!"

"Do not underestimate the ancients and their arts. Of course, they did not use the word *science*, and they did not carry their food around in plastic containers, but their finest minds shaped their world using the basic raw materials that were at their disposal. I am talking about earth, water, wind and fire. Dottore Richards, the Romans were *brilliant* wind engineers!"

"Then why do we not know of their achievements? Why has their knowledge and their discoveries not been passed down to us?"

"Much, I am afraid to say, was buried in ash on the slopes of Mount Vesuvius, not far from here, many centuries ago."

"In Pompeii, in 79 AD?"

A faint smile spread among the old man's wrinkles.

"Well, this is just fantastic!" exclaimed Richards. "How can I get hold of this information?"

"Careful, Dottore," cautioned the old man in a hushed voice, raising the palm of his right hand. "I do not want to say too much, as I don't know who else might be listening. But I am sure that if you go to the place that you have just mentioned, you will find proof of what I have just told you. What is more, I am sure that it will all seem very familiar to you."

Richards was so excited at the prospect of such new discoveries that he did not question how the old man knew this information, nor did he wonder at the reason for the frail but alert gentleman's caution. Frantically, his mind searched for ideas as to what gaps in knowledge the ancient Romans might be able to fill, but his attention was brought back to the present by the feel of the old man's cold, dry hand on his forearm.

"*Chiaroscuro. Chiaroscuro.* Shades of darkness will come to your foreground if you don't look out for the lighter shades in your background," he said.

There was silence as Richards stared into the man's eyes, which appeared impenetrable in the half-light of the restaurant. The old man ended the pause with another question. "Did you think to look at the other side of the card, Dottore?"

Richards gazed at the card:

THE SATOR MAGIC SQUARE

On the other side it had:

Richards turned over the card, and the bright colours of two of Caravaggio's best-known paintings stood out in the candlelight. "Yes, they're paintings—by Caravaggio."

The old man said nothing, his gaze fixed on Richards. His weatherworn face betrayed a slight smile, which encouraged the young engineer to explore the paintings more deeply.

"They are painted in a Baroque style, which Caravaggio sort of pioneered and others followed. One of the paintings is of the head of John the Baptist, and—"

"A true leader enters into his own destiny with fortitude and finds his own pathway. Look more closely."

Richards studied the two paintings, peering at every detail, analysing the face of each character, searching for imagery that might betray some meaning. At length, he looked up from the card. The old man was no longer there.

Richards sat back in the chair astonished. He contemplated everything that the man had said to him. *What is the meaning of "chiaroscuro," and what message might be hidden in the paintings?*

Richards made his way back to Rossini, who was sitting alone, accompanied only by his second martini, a Campari that matched the colour of her blouse, and a complimentary bowl of olives.

"What was all that about? A friend of yours?" Rossini asked.

Richards took his seat without saying anything at first. After carefully measuring his words he said, "Well, not exactly. He's someone who I met for the first time at the seminar, this afternoon. In fact, I don't even know the gentleman's name."

Ben then showed Rossini the card and shared with her everything he could remember about what Father Luigi had told him about sator squares the previous evening. She also examined the paintings in great detail.

"These are both very famous paintings, Ben," she said, "and they are very familiar to people in this part of Italy. You will know that Caravaggio was very much a local painter. In fact, you will probably find that prints of both of the paintings on this card will be displayed here in the restaurant."

"Yes, I know," Richards replied. "But I'm sure that the old fella was trying to draw my attention to something important in these paintings . . . I just can't see it."

Their conversation was interrupted by the sound of a glass breaking on the hard stone floor behind the bar.

"Oops!" cried Richards. "That's one glass that the barman won't need to wash."

"True," Rossini giggled. "But I hate to hear a glass break like that."

"Why?"

"I don't know," she said, raising her own glass to the light of the candle and examining its form. The Campari, which had previously appeared to be blood red, in the half-light now became very translucent, and the rough-hewn ice cubes that drifted gently just below the surface reflected and dispersed the intense candlelight. "I think it's because a glass is something perfect when it is whole, but so very fragile. Once it breaks, it can never be repaired, rather like a life. Don't you think?"

Ben was captivated by the young woman, astonished by the beauty of the sentiment that she had just expressed. He fixed upon dark-brown eyes that invited a response he felt unable to articulate.

"I suppose there are many things that cannot be retrieved, once they are lost," he muttered.

Rossini smiled sympathetically, realising that there was more to Ben's words than he was prepared to explain.

"Excuse me, signor," said a young waiter who, quite unnoticed, had approached the table and was anxiously waiting for an opportunity to interrupt the couple. "I am sorry, signor, but you are Dottore *Reeshards*?" he asked.

"Si. That's me."

"Well, were you expecting to meet a lady this evening?"

Rossini shot Richards a wicked glare before rescuing him from embarrassment.

"Si. *Vabene*." She smiled. She then said something else in Italian with more smiles, which Ben did not understand but which clearly brought complete relief to the young man. After delivering his message in his native tongue, Rossini turned to Ben.

"It appears that German *Herman* will not be joining you tonight."

"Will you be wanting to order now?" asked the waiter.

The couple had barely started to peruse the antipasti menu when Richards' attention shifted in the direction of the table the old man had occupied just minutes earlier. To his surprise, the sound of a match was followed by the illumination of a face that had recently become familiar to him—the unmistakeable figure of the man who approached him in the apartment the previous day. *Merisi.*

The bearded man very pointedly cast his eyes towards Ben's smartphone, which was in front of him on the table. At that very moment, a text message appeared.

Chiaroscuro, it said.

"What is it?" asked Rossini. Before Ben could respond his smartphone pinged again with the words, *LEAVE NOW.*

Richards stood.

"Grazia, we need to go . . . now!"

CHAPTER 20

REVELATIONS

Without a moment's hesitation, Rossini put down her menu and gathered up her handbag. Richards picked up his phone and the two quickly stepped towards the exit hand in hand.

Ben's phone illuminated again, and he heard a voice that he recognised immediately. It was Merisi.

"Do not draw attention to yourself, Dottore, by hurrying. Just make your way out of the restaurant, but do not use the main doors that you used when you arrived; use the side door that opens out onto the Via Conte."

"What is going on? And how are you speaking to me on my phone without me accepting the call?"

"There is no time to explain. Just make your way out of the restaurant, and I will try to meet you outside. Can you see the door I am referring to? The single door, not the double door."

"Yes, I can see it," Richards answered. Rossini looked frightened as he guided her like a parent gently pulling on the arm of a small child.

"It's this way," he said, leading her between crimson-covered tables towards the opposite side of the restaurant, still holding the phone to his ear.

"There is no more time for puzzles and riddles, Dottore. I have been showing you paintings with clues hidden in them, hoping that you would discover the messages for yourself. You have to be aware of what is going on around you. Your background has ears and eyes."

"What? You mean to say that I am being—"

"Be aware, Dottore; be very aware. You yourself are in a painting with your competition watching you."

As Merisi articulated the word *painting*, Richard's attention was drawn to a self-portrait of Caravaggio on the restaurant wall. The way in which the artist's face seemed to be illuminated by the vivid oils against the dark background reminded Richards of the way in which Merisi had attracted his attention just minutes earlier. What intrigued Richards most was the remarkable likeness between the two men—the goatee beard, the dishevelled hair and the stern expression.

"We are running out of time. I think they are onto us," Merisi said.

"But what do you mean by *messages*?"

"Caravaggio was known for his revolutionary style of painting, and for the hidden messages that were contained within them."

"What hidden messages?"

"He allowed his central figures to emerge from the darkness, powerfully illuminating them as if by a spotlight, while the rest of the scene remained mysteriously in the shadows."

Richards pressed the phone closer to his ear, anxious to hear every word.

"You said, 'They are onto us.' Who is 'they'?"

"Androids!"

Richards shuddered as Merisi paused on the other end of the phone.

"Advanced, humanoid machines," continued Merisi. "But they are incapable of understanding the psychological, philosophical and emotional messages conveyed in paintings, which is why I have used the paintings to send you messages that you can understand but they cannot."

"And what am I supposed to glean from his paintings?" Richards asked.

"Shades of darkness will come to your foreground if you don't look out for the lighter shades in your background. The lighter shades in the background represent a threat to you from your competitors, which can prevent your ideas from becoming active in the foreground," explained Merisi.

Richards did not immediately grasp what Merisi was trying to tell him. "Go on," he said, pausing just a few feet in front of door.

"And Caravaggio's *The Supper at Emmaus*," Merisi continued. "What that means is that you have the power to open the eyes of others; they know you, and then you vanish. You have revealed your true identity, but have others? Are there other leaders with vision who can develop, carry and deliver ideas in the same way that you can?

"Your appearance at the seminar resembles the last supper. The disciples in the painting resemble your panel and audience. You, like Christ, are preaching your word. The painting tells us that Christ is only there for the supper, in the same way that you are only there for the seminar. That means that your ideas may be taken forward by somebody else who is present. You will know that Christ disappears, and so might you, and your ideas might fall into the wrong hands if you are not careful."

The information was too much for Richards to take in, so he stood transfixed for several moments and said nothing.

"Ben!" exclaimed Rossini, impatiently squeezing and shaking the engineer's hand.

"Yes, of course," he replied, and opened the door onto the street. The warmth of the restaurant gave way to a sudden freshness as rain fell heavily on the cobbled pavement outside.

Merisi immediately noticed the noisy downpour in the background.

"So, you are outside, now, Dottore?"

"Yes."

"You need to cross the street, now, and then make your way to the main square. I will tell you where to go after that."

Richards followed Merisi's instructions and led Grazia across the rain-soaked street.

"So, what is the plan, Merisi? Where do we go from here?"

"What is important now is that you get to Pompeii as soon as you can."

The noise of the rain hammering on the street and on the row of cars parked there made Merisi's voice seem more distant.

"What? Pompeii? As in the ruins?"

"Yes, Pompeii. And you must be vigilant and watch out for people who may not be what they at first seem. But I have given you something to help you with that."

As Merisi spoke, the summer storm intensified, making his voice no more than a whisper.

"What? I can barely hear you in this storm. You say you've given me something? What have you given me? Hello . . ."

At that moment, Richards became aware of the roar of a car's engine and, to his horror, turned his head to see a metallic-green sports car on the pavement heading straight at him. Rossini screamed, and there was a shrill screeching of brakes as the car broadsided and knocked Richards to the ground, sending his phone skidding into the shallow gutter.

Struggling to regain his senses as he lay on the saturated ground, Richards became aware of the sound of car doors opening and closing, of men frantically shouting orders in Italian, and then of Rossini's desperate screams. As he rose to his knees, behind him he heard her cries for help suddenly become muffled, before a final slamming of a car door and the roar of an engine as the vehicle sped away.

Richards watched the Audi disappear. Now soaked to the skin and unaware of where his phone had gone, he felt utterly helpless. At that moment, a second sports car pulled up. This time it was a white, open-topped convertible. Richards was surprised to see that the roof on the car was down despite the pouring rain. But what amazed him most was that it was driven by the beautiful, raven-haired Italian woman who was the very reason for him being at Caravaggio's that evening. Swiftly and athletically, the woman leapt from the car and approached Richards.

"Someone's taken Grazia! They went that way," he said.

"Do not concern yourself with her, Doctor *Ree*-chards. She has gone. There is nothing that you can do about that now."

Suddenly, Richards became hypersensitive to everything around him. He was aware of the sights and sounds and smells all at once, yet he had the ability to distinguish between each of them. Each individual drop of rain. The sound of many vehicles and voices, some of them far away. He heard every syllable, every footstep of passers-by, and the swish of cars' tyres on the wet tarmac of streets in the distance.

"Come with me, Doctor *Ree*-chards. I will look after you," said the woman, inviting Richards into the car.

Richards noticed the echo of each raindrop dancing on the white leather seats within, and he was aware of the difference in pitch that they made compared with the rain falling on the surrounding streets. Colours, too, appeared to be heightened in a way that he could not begin to describe. He looked in wonder at the way the neon signs of the restaurant and the brilliant white of the nearby streetlights reflected from the polished exterior of the car. They bombarded his senses with more colours than he knew existed.

Stranger still, when he switched his gaze to the woman who stood before him, her features became blurred, her silhouette appeared to shimmer slightly, and then Richards perceived her very clearly as being a lean, extremely fit man of Chinese descent. What was even stranger was that Richards somehow knew that the person who stood before him, smiling, was genetically 68 percent Chinese, 10 percent Japanese, 10 percent West European, and 12 percent of something altogether different. At the same time, he knew that this stranger was 88 percent male and 12 percent something else.

"Why you look at me like that, Doctor *Ree*-chards? You like the dress? Oh, I think you are undressing me with your eyes, no?"

Richards said nothing but continued to gaze at the being in front of him with amazement. Suddenly, Shui Feng's expression shifted to one of cold determination.

"Yes, I think you certainly need to come with me now, Richards."

With that, he removed a small, glass phial from his tunic and sprayed a fine mist in Richards' face. Again, Richards was aware of even the smallest individual droplet and, it seemed, molecule of the liquid as it hit his skin. His heightened olfactory senses also detected each constituent chemical that made up the compound, and each appeared familiar to him.

The street around him suddenly rotated, and he felt himself being lifted off his feet by a pair of immensely strong arms. The next thing Richards knew, he was sitting in the reclined passenger seat of the car, with his sodden clothes feeling cold against his skin and sticking to the wet, white leather. Feng was now looking down on him, keenly observing Richards' dilated pupils.

"Sleep, Dr. Richards," he said with a smile that was neither kindly nor reassuring. "I am going to take care of you."

Ben's last thought was of Grazia Rossini's desperate cries for help. Then consciousness began to fade as the faint sound of the car stereo played: *"Different colours, different shades. Over each mistakes were made. I took the blame. Directionless so plain to see, A loaded gun won't set you free."*

Then all went dark.

ACKNOWLEDGMENTS

Thank you to my ghostwriter, Dr. Philip Barham. Without his significant contribution as a ghostwriter, this story would not have been completed.

Thank you to publisher Malcolm Down, my running friend at Milton Keynes Athletic Club, for finding Dr. Mark Stibbe, who contributed to help ghostwrite the story initially. Thank you to both novelist Bryony Pearce and Chloe, a professional reader who worked for Malcolm Down, in giving me their feedback to help me make necessary improvements.

Thank you to Israel Oba, a marketer, for finding Lisa Strobl, a screenplay writer who helped me find Koehler Books and without whom this book would not have been published.

Thank you to Dennis Woods from Koehler Books for finding an interest in my story and considering it for publishing, and thank you dearly to the team at Koehler Books; John Koehler for believing in my story, and Danielle Kohler for her support in marketing the book, and Joe Coccaro for the editing of the story.

Thank you to Pete Moran and Jamie Noble for their creativity and execution in producing the digital graphic illustrations for the story.

Most of all, thank you to my wife, Jacqueline, and my son, Ethan, who have gave me their full support, belief, and understanding to help me find myself.

CPSIA information can be obtained
at www.ICGtesting.com
Printed in the USA
LVHW040841300919
632673LV00001B/75/P